"Cary Herwig's *The World Ends at the River* perfectly captures the languid summer days in the South of the 1950s. You feel the sticky heat, hear the drone of bees, see the lightning bugs at night...and you also feel deeply for the protagonist, a young girl on the verge of womanhood who discovers her family's unearthly inheritance and the consequences that it brings   I kept turning page after page... and I will be waiting eagerly for the next installment. Highly recommended."

— KATHRYN PTACEK, AUTHOR OF *SHADOWEYES* AND EDITOR OF *WOMEN OF DARKNESS*

"*The Ghost's Daughter* by Cary Herwig is a suspense-filled novel that held my attention throughout. This novel took me back to the 1950s when society expected women to be seen and not heard....I loved Vivien's courage and dedication to her family. Thank you for this captivating story,

—JENNIFER IBIAM, *READERS' FAVORITE*

"Hysteria. What else could it be? At Camp Breckenridge in 1956, Vivien is continually drawn to an abandoned hospital where she encounters something bizarre and terrifying. This book pulled me back to a simpler time and kept me on the edge of my seat. The characters were lifelike and the danger was real. It kept me turning the pages to find out what happens next."

THE WORLD ENDS AT THE RIVER

THE WORLD ENDS AT THE RIVER

THE ARMY BRAT HAUNTINGS
BOOK TWO

CARY HERWIG

CHAPTER
ONE

May 1957, Manchester, Tennessee

The chicken's clucking echoed under the old metal washtub. The tub sat upside down with the rim hanging slightly over the edge of the wooden porch so the hen got air but couldn't escape. Grandma caught the chicken yesterday and it had been a full day, enough time for her to clean herself out, meaning the chicken shit all over the boards. Grandma — or more likely Vivien — would wash it off with the hose later.

Vivien went out on the porch right after breakfast and sat on one of the cane-bottom chairs. She leaned it back against the wall on two legs and watched the trees behind the place sway in the wind, the leaves glittering in the sunlight. She hadn't yet figured out what they said, but one day the words would be plain to her ear.

Grandma had told her to "stay there 'cause I'm goin' to teach you how to wring a chicken's neck. All girls should know how." She'd seen Grandma do it plenty of times and had no desire to take up the practice.

She sat forward, putting all four legs of the chair on the boards. She'd been dreading this ever since getting out of bed and being told today was the day. Grandma, who'd killed chickens to cook for supper all of her life, didn't understand her reluctance. There must be a place to hide until Grandma got tired of waiting and took care of it herself.

Her mother and Lauren, her sister, were off visiting Daddy's family for a couple of weeks. Daddy shipped out to France last fall, posted at a place called Fontenet, and planned to take the whole family across the Atlantic come September. She doubted she would need this particular talent over there.

Vivien stayed with Grandma so she could learn a few things. Mama and Grandma cooked up the idea between them. They figured Grandma could teach her a lot about the family's background and about being a grown woman. Vivien understood what Mama wanted, but Grandma's old-fashioned ideas didn't work in the modern, mid-1950s world. Wringing a chicken's neck didn't seem to be required much when Mama went to the supermarket and bought one already killed and plucked. However, they made the decision and she found herself stuck with it.

"She's ready, Vivien," Grandma called out.

She came out the back door from the kitchen, letting the wooden screen door slam behind her.

Grandma lifted the washtub a bit and reached under it. In a moment, her hand reappeared, fingers wrapped around the hen's neck.

"Now, you just take hold of the neck like this and spin her until the head comes off."

"Aw, Grandma. I don't want to."

"You want fried chicken for dinner tonight?"

She made the best fried chicken in the whole world and, yes, Vivien wanted it for dinner. But . . .

"Do like I say. Grab hold of the neck. Hold tight. And twirl it around like you seen me do."

"It'll hurt her."

"Nah, happens too fast. She won't feel a thing."

Vivien knew better, but you don't argue with your grandma. Not much, anyway. Vivien contemplated grabbing the feathered neck. What if the hen pecked her? Well, it would be hard for her to do, wouldn't it? She imagined the eyes popping out of her head from the pressure of the hand. There'd be blood. The saying, "running around like a chicken with its head chopped off," wasn't just a saying. She'd seen more than one running around headless before.

"Go on."

Vivien wrapped her fingers around the scrawny neck, and Grandma slid her hand free. Closing her eyes, Vivien tightened her hold and twirled the poor creature around. Suddenly it felt light as a feather. She looked down. In her hand, drops of blood dripped from the chicken's neck. She screamed and threw the head to the ground.

The rest of the hen ran around on those scrawny feet, heading for the corner of the house.

"Quick, grab it before it runs into the road."

Vivien took off after it. It disappeared around the corner. It flopped up and down in the grass at the side of the house. She'd never seen one do that before. Blood flew from its neck, down its feathers onto the grass and upward onto the mostly unpainted wall of the house.

She pounced on it and held it to the ground. Its muscles contracted, then became still. Grandma came around the corner and Vivien looked up.

"Well, I never," she said, looking from the wall to the dead bird.

Vivien looked from Grandma to the wall. Drops of blood ran down the clapboard siding.

"I ain't never seen one bleed so much."

"Look, Grandma."

"What?"

"The blood on the wall."

She came closer and looked up, shrieked, and covered her mouth with her hand.

"Oh, my Lord," she said reverently.

The blood spatter ran into the shape of a face. The hair long, down to where the shoulders would be. Eyes, nose, cheeks, jaw, beard. It was all there.

It looked exactly like Jesus.

CHAPTER
TWO

"Well, I don't know, Opal Lee."

Brother Richard Davis, pastor at Grandma's church, looked at the picture on the wall for several minutes. He walked up and down, squatted on his heels, got up, backed up, moved close, and looked at it from all angles. Every so often he said, "Hm," profoundly.

Brother Davis, short and overweight, always wore a suit, never a hat, and always spoke as if delivering a sermon. In spite of his size and oration, he rarely ever sweat, no matter how hot it got.

"It does resemble the pictures mightily." Framed prints depicting Jesus hung in the church. He liked the word, "mightily" a lot, using it in his sermons several times each Sunday.

"Should I wash it off?" Grandma asked.

"Have you told anyone else about it?"

"No. No, I didn't want to be disrespectful."

Brother Davis nodded. Grandma lived in rural Coffee County, deep in the hills of Middle Tennessee. People there were often superstitious, although not so deep in the back

5

country they didn't know about manifestations in other parts. Most of those were Catholic and of no account to the Baptists they knew. Others were just foreign, so they had no real bearing on anything, either. This, however, appeared in their backyard, both literally and figuratively.

"For the time being, I suggest you put a sheet or something over it, so others can't see it. That road . . ." He pointed at the dirt road, running about fifteen feet below the edge of the property, in a sharp curve. "People might see it from their cars down there."

Vivien wondered how many had already seen it, since the picture had been there most of the day. A dirt road it might be, but it could be pretty busy at times, with farmers and others going back and forth between town and home. The school lay in the same direction, but not much traffic headed there during summer vacation. Usually, people went there to make repairs and get the building ready for the new school year.

No harm would come to it, except maybe rain. Grandma went inside to fetch an old sheet, and the pastor helped her bring out the ladder. They leaned it against the house, and he climbed up with a hammer and a few nails she handed to him, while holding onto a corner of the sheet. Stretching it out, he pounded a nail through one corner of the muslin, then another and another across the top edge. Before long, the sheet hung over the holy, or unholy, likeness. He left in his brand new Chevy pickup, promising to talk to other pastors and do some praying to figure out what to do.

Brother Davis never called and, on Sunday, the two of them dutifully dressed up in their Sunday-go-to-meetin' best. They got to church a little early, Grandma carried her Bible, like always. People stood around talking, but when they saw the two of them, they grew quiet.

Uh oh, I think the cat is out of the bag.

Mrs. Trent came up to Grandma, looking stern.

"Why did you cover up the picture of the Lord Jesus on the side of the house? It's blasphemy."

Grandma looked startled. She seemed to find it hard to believe Mrs. Trent not only knew about it, but thought she had a say in the matter. Looking at the faces of the ladies talking with Mrs. Trent, it appeared everyone knew and had an opinion. Manchester being a small town, deep in Baptist country, people not only knew everyone else's business, they knew what was right and didn't mind telling you.

"Brother Davis thought it best while we're trying to figure out what to do about it."

"It's your house, Opal Lee. Your decision."

"Yes, it is."

Grandma's chin went up and her eyes squinted. She put her hand behind Vivien's shoulder and guided her to their usual seats.

A podium stood on the raised dais at the far end. The small church building had few decorations in accordance with Baptist beliefs, and a small congregation, mostly farmers with little money. The sun shone brightly through plain windows

Their regular pew being near the front, much of the congregation sat behind them. Vivien felt eyes boring into the back of her head. She turned around, but Grandma put her hand on her chin and turned her to face front.

A woman played the piano, a member of the congregation whose name Vivien could never remember. A murmur of voices rose and fell, seeming in time with the music. One of the pictures of Jesus looked over the gathering from off to one side. Although having more detail, the similarity to the hen's blood picture couldn't be denied.

Brother Davis came onto the dais from a side door, followed by two men she'd never seen before. The reverend placed his open Bible on the podium. Looking out over the small crowd, he smiled and raised his hands, indicating everyone should rise for the first hymn. The two strangers stepped down to the front pew to the right. They also wore suits, one similar to Brother Davis's. The third man wore a light beige expensive-looking suit. One of them sang off-key but with gusto.

Brother Davis based his sermon on miracles. Grandma muttered beside her. He spoke a lot about how Jesus comes to us when we need him, but there are times he comes just because we love him. The service wound down and Brother Davis asked everyone to stay behind for a meeting.

Would he talk about the picture? It seemed to be on people's minds. Grandma seemed worried. The final hymn ended, and everyone sat back down instead of making their way toward the door. Vivien worried about being sent outside, but Grandma said nothing, staring straight ahead. Grandma sniffed, like she did when she was upset. Vivien didn't understand what upset her.

People whispered while Brother Davis stepped down to talk with the two strangers. The three of them went up on the stage and Brother Davis motioned for quiet.

"It seems many people have seen the bloodstain on the wall of Opal Lee Flynn's house in the county. If you haven't seen it yourself, you've heard about it. Sister Opal Lee called me yesterday when it happened, and I went out to look it over. She worried whether to allow it to wash away in the next rain, or if she should wash it off herself, or if it might be important enough to protect. We covered it with a sheet for the time being."

People nodded and whispers rose again. Brother Davis cleared his throat and continued. He described how the face of Jesus came to be on the house. A woman asked if "the little girl" wrung the hen's neck. A man asked what happened to the hen.

"We ate it," Grandma said when the pastor looked to her to answer. People gasped, chuckled, and voices rose, asking a number of questions. Brother Davis raised his hand for quiet.

"Seems sensible," he said. "Now, I've invited Brother Grayson and Brother Adair to come to discuss what should be done. Brother Grayson, as many of you know, is pastor at the First Baptist Church over in Tullahoma. Brother Adair is a pillar of our community who has made donations to keep our church in good repair. They have consented to lend their voices to our deliberations. The three of us have discussed the event among ourselves, but we wanted to give everyone a chance to have a say."

"Wait a minute." Grandma stood. Her hands rested on the back of the pew in front of her. "This is my house we're talking about, and the final choice is mine."

"Of course," Brother Davis said, and the other men nodded soberly.

She stood for another moment but said nothing else. She sat down. Her jaw muscles twitched as if she clenched her teeth to keep herself silent.

The next few minutes the pastors expressed their joy and appreciation for the honor visited on the community in general, and Grandma in particular. She harumphed and almost missed their calling "the little girl" particularly blessed. The first time she killed a chicken and look what happened. Grandma patted Vivien's hand she'd put on her grandma's arm.

Maybe they were about to see the Rapture, or something else equally life changing. "Grandma?"

"It's all right," Grandma whispered. "The world ain't ending quite yet."

One of the men — she couldn't remember their names — said our "good Baptist beliefs" didn't usually include such exhibits of devotion — unlike the Catholics — but this moment couldn't be ignored. The men on the stage believed they must preserve and protect the image.

Mrs. Trent spoke up. "God and Jesus, His Son, sent this image to us. He shed his blood for our sins, and this is a symbol of his sacrifice."

She went on for a spell, then others spoke. Most agreed with Mrs. Trent. Many wanted to pray under that gaze and wanted others to have the same opportunity. Vivien imagined a horde of people trampling Grandma's grass so they could kneel, lifting up their eyes to admire the blood image.

She kept thinking of it as chicken blood, spread randomly by a dying bird. How could they think it holy? And how would they protect it from washing away in the next rain?

Someone raised the same question, and they all talked over each other. She didn't hear it all, so didn't understand what they considered the final solution. Grandma shook her head. When the next silence descended, she rose.

"All of this talk and no one has asked me if I want to preserve this image on my house. Brother Davis, I asked for your advice, but I did not say you or anyone else could choose what would be done about this."

A man behind agreed with her. "It's her house," he said.

Several voices rose, speaking over each other, again.

Vivien looked over her shoulder at the people behind them. Familiar faces, a few slightly remembered. Strong emotions showed on all, mouths opening and closing. One woman raised her Bible and spoke, her voice blending with the others. They quieted, and she turned to see Brother Davis holding up his hand.

"There's time to decide what to do," he said. "We don't want to stir up any hard feelings among us."

They bowed their heads while he spoke the blessing and made his way down the center aisle toward the door. The other preacher and the man in the beige suit huddled together on the stage, talking, ignoring the rest of them. Members of the congregation filed out, voices debating the issue. Grandma continued to stand there, rigid and staring straight ahead. Most of the people had passed when she finally relaxed and moved to the aisle.

Mrs. Trent stood near the door watching them approach. She and Grandma never seemed close, but they'd always been friendly.

"Don't do anything uncalled for," Mrs. Trent called out. They kept walking.

Grandma walked past Brother Davis without shaking his hand. Usually she stood outside, talking to others she knew. Today, they got in the car and drove home.

CHAPTER
THREE

Grandma drove her old Ford into the gravel driveway beside the house and slammed to a stop. Cars lined the side of the dirt road. A gathering of people stood in her yard on the far side.

Vivien jumped out of the car to follow Grandma who practically ran around the house in her sensible shoes. The sheet hung by one corner, revealing the picture. A few people knelt on the ground, all clearly praying. One woman sobbed.

"Get out!"

All eyes turned to Grandma. Most were strangers. So many faces filled with strong emotions and feelings. Anger, sorrow, even pleading. No one could predict what they might do, but not one of them moved.

"Go away!" Grandma shouted.

When none of them moved, she turned and stalked into the house. Vivien stood fixed to the spot, wondering what to do. Grandma came back out, carrying Grandpa's old rabbit ears shotgun. It hadn't been fired in decades. No telling if she'd loaded it or knew how to fire it. If she pulled the trigger, would it actually fire? Or would it blow up?

The crowd of people didn't know either. The kneeling ones stood. The praying ones lowered their hands. Their feet shuffled in the grass and took them toward their cars parked along the dirt road. It took a while for all of them to move, and the whole time Grandma stood waving the shotgun at them, shouting for them to leave.

When they'd gone, she lowered the barrel toward the ground and took a deep breath. "Let's have lunch."

They ate leftover fried chicken, cole slaw, and fresh corn from her garden. They cleaned up the dishes, then Vivien went outside to play. She loved the old rope swing hanging from the walnut tree in the front yard and could get way up high in it. When she did, she could see pretty far down the road that formed a Y with the road past the house. Before long, she saw several cars headed their way, raising a cloud of dust. Four or five of them. When they turned into the driveway, she stopped the swing and watched people climb out.

Men and women came toward her; several held up cameras and snapped pictures of her and the house. She slid out of the swing and watched them close in on her.

"Are you the little girl who is responsible for the picture of Jesus?" one woman asked.

They surrounded her.

"I'm not a little girl," she shouted, her voice trembling.

"Vivien!"

Grandma rushed out the front door of the house, carrying the shotgun again. Vivien wanted to run over to her, but the people hemmed her in.

"Hold on," one of the men said. "We don't mean any harm. I'm from the *Coffee County Times* and these other folks are from other newspapers. We only want your side of the story."

Grandma continued walking toward them, holding the shotgun steady. "Move aside," she said as she came up, and they shuffled to let her through their circle to stand beside her granddaughter. She nodded to Vivien, as if to say, "You're all right. I'm here."

Vivien stood against her. She loved Grandma and trusted her, at that moment, more than ever.

The reporters snapped more pictures and called out questions.

"Exactly when did this happen?"

"The child did it, right?"

"What do you intend doing with it?"

"Have you spoken with anyone for advice?"

"What church do you attend?"

Grandma held the gun pointed at one and another in turn.

"Leave us in peace," she said. "We have nothing to say."

"But people want to know about this Jesus picture and what's going to happen to it."

"That's my business," she said.

They kept shouting questions, and she kept telling them to leave. A couple of them moved away, toward the side of the house, their cameras at the ready.

"Move away from there," Grandma called out. "I'll call the sheriff."

They left, grumbling about freedom of the press and the public's right to know. "Let's go inside. I'm too tired today, but tomorrow, I'm taking the hose to the thing. Can't let this go on until it becomes a misery."

She tucked Vivien into bed early. Vivien turned on the lamp beside the bed and reached for her book. She fell asleep after half an hour or so, the book lying on her chest.

A loud, vibrating sound woke her. She jerked awake,

confusing dream with what she heard. In another moment Grandma called her name.

"What is it, Grandma?"

"Stay in your room," she shouted.

Vivien heard her moving around when the growling stopped for a moment, then the noise returned, drowning out any other sounds. She jumped out of bed, put on her slippers and robe, and raced to the back porch. Stepping off into the grass, she saw Grandma heading toward the side of the house, no shotgun in sight. Vivien ran after, curiosity propelling her, plus a desire to face the trouble with her grandma.

Grandma stopped dead in her tracks. Vivien came up behind her and did the same.

Three men stood there, one with a power saw in his hands, one with a powerful flashlight, and the third who seemed to be watching. This man walked over to Grandma.

"What do you men think you're doing? This is my house."

"We can't let you destroy this," the man said.

Grandma stepped toward the man with the saw and the other man grabbed her and held her arms tight against her sides. The man with the saw went back to work in the light of the flashlight. In the dark, Vivien recognized the man holding onto Grandma from church. Mr. Adair. He'd stood on the dais with Brother Davis. Brother Davis held the flashlight, while the preacher from Tullahoma, also seen that morning with the others, wielded the chainsaw to cut around the hen's blood picture.

"Be quiet, Opal Lee," Brother Davis called out.

Vivien kicked the man holding Grandma as hard as she could in slippers, and he bent over, rubbing his shin. Grandma took a step toward her pastor and the man grabbed her again. He looked down at Vivien.

"Kick me again, and I'll hurt her," he said.

She didn't believe him, but the world had stopped being what she knew. She wouldn't take any chances on his doing what he said.

Grandma stopped struggling. For the first time, she looked old and tired, and it made Vivien more afraid. She hated these men as she'd never hated before. They hurt Grandma physically. They were also hurting her pride and sense of independence and strength.

The man with the saw worked away, cutting out the section of the wall with the picture of Jesus in hen's blood. The whole thing measured about five by six feet when they pulled it away from the house. The hole revealed plaster underneath, crumbling to the ground.

The man holding Grandma pushed her away. "Go into the house, Ms. Flynn."

Instead, she turned to Brother Davis. "How could you do this to one of your own?"

"We'll put this up on the wall of our church. We'll become famous throughout the state," he said. "Our picture will be in papers all over."

"You mean *your* picture will."

He shrugged. Vivien had just been introduced to runaway ambition. It looked pretty ugly.

They watched the three men carry the section of wall to the driveway toward a flatbed truck. They struggled to lift it up onto the truck bed.

When they finally got the picture loaded, they drove off and Grandma went inside and called the sheriff. The clock striking three was the last thing Vivien heard before she fell asleep on the sofa. The screen door slammed and woke her. Afterward, she vaguely remembered Sheriff Jameson's voice and that of his woman deputy and Grandma talking in the kitchen. She fell back asleep, wondering about a sheriff having a woman for a deputy.

The sheriff arrested the three men the next day and confiscated the section of the wall. The men were released the day after. The insurance company adjuster came out to check the wall and see if the policy covered the damage. They classified it as vandalism, so they covered the cost of repair, but he said they would sue the men "to recoup the loss." Men came out later and tacked a tarp over the hole to keep out the weather until it could be fixed. Thank goodness it hadn't rained for a week.

Grandma called Mama long distance and told her what happened and suggested they come back and get Vivien. She didn't want to leave, and it hurt that Grandma didn't want her there.

"I'm sorry, Grandma. It's all my fault. I didn't wring the chicken's neck right."

Grandma pulled her to her ample bosom and rocked her.

"It's not your fault, sweetie. You did it exactly right. The world went crazy for a little while. Too many people just can't let others live their lives."

A fragment of the conversation on the phone with Mama came to mind. Grandma talked about living alone. "Lots of widows are on their own," Grandma had said. "We all have to be careful of those who want what we have."

She talked about the land of the farm and how someone in Manchester wanted it. "Just because I'm a widow, that doesn't mean they can just come in and take it."

No threats of violence were ever made against her, but every so often, trespassers appeared. Once, surveyors brought their equipment and she ran them off.

"It's been a long time since I've been bothered, but I 'spect all of this will make it easy for them to be after me, again."

Grandma's fears made Vivien want to stay with her. Leaving her alone wasn't right.

Mama and Lauren planned to be gone another week. They'd either have to come back early, or she'd have to take a bus to join them. She preferred to stay and help. Grandma agreed she didn't want to be alone. They called Mama back, and she agreed Vivien could stay, making her promise not to get in the way.

The days passed. Men came and repaired the wall. No one ever told them what happened to the hen's blood Jesus, but people more than likely made money off the thing. They sure didn't want it because they thought it was pretty.

Until Mama and Lauren came back, they ate vegetables from the garden, bacon, and sausages. If anything looked even remotely Christ-like, they didn't mention it.

FOUR

A week after Mama and Lauren got back to Grandma's, Mama announced she wanted to take a ride in the car. The Chevy sat idle the whole time the two of them visited Daddy's relatives. Vivien had started it every day, but it could use a good run.

It was wash day, which always began early in hopes they would finish before the day heated up. The two of them hung the wet clothes on the line.

"Where are we going?" Vivien asked. After being confined to Grandma's and church, going on an outing sounded great.

"I want to visit Camp Forrest," Mama said. "I'd like to see what's left."

A twinge of fear rushed through Vivien. She swallowed hard, remembering her encounter with the ghost of Nurse Armstrong at Camp Breckinridge, where they lived before coming to Grandma's. She'd threatened not only her, but her whole family.

"What is it?" Vivien asked.

"It's the post where your father was stationed when we

met. He came into the Owl Café on the square one afternoon where I worked. I waited on him, and we got to talking. The second time he came in, he asked me out." Mama smiled. "We could only go to the movies, at first. Later, we went to the enlisted club on post." She shook out another sheet to hang on the line. "I thought I'd told you all about it."

"I remember you worked at the Owl, but I don't remember Camp Forrest." She did remember Daddy being stationed near Manchester, but the name of the camp rang no bells. "I don't think I want to go."

"Of course, you do. You've been cooped up here at Grandma's for over four weeks, except for Sundays." She put a clothes pin in her mouth for the next corner of the sheet but took it out and studied Vivien. "Are you afraid?"

"No."

Mama's eyebrows went up.

"It's just . . . It's okay. I'll go."

Vivien picked up the empty laundry basket and carried it to the porch, where she set it down beside the wringer washing machine. The old bushel basket needed a new liner, but they hadn't made a point of buying one yet.

The idea of being so close to another old army post worried her. What if she saw another ghost there? When they left Breckinridge, she'd hoped she'd never see another one, ever.

The agitator worked back and forth, the water in the tub frothy with Tide soap powder. She sat in the old rocking chair and in a moment rocked in time with the washer. Swish-swish, swish-swish. Mama checked the machine and patted Vivien's shoulder. She lowered the drain hose to drain the soapy water down the hill. They fed each piece of clothing through the wringer and re-filled the tub with rinse water. When the rinse finished, Mama ran each item through the wringer again and handed it to Vivien who shook it out and put it in the basket.

After they finished hanging up everything, Mama said, "I'm going to write a letter to your daddy when we're done. Want me to tell him anything?"

"Yes, ma'am. I look forward to his coming to get us." By the time he did, it would be a year since she'd seen him.

Mama went inside, coming out in a few minutes with a glass of sweet tea. She handed it to Vivien and went back inside. Vivien passed the dripping glass across her forehead like she'd seen Mama do many times. The coolness felt good but wet. She pulled up the hem of her shirt and wiped away water and her own sweat.

She loved being with Grandma, who surely must be lonely when they weren't there. Grandpa died before Vivien came along. Years ago, all of her other seven children — Vivien's aunts, uncles, and cousins — had moved out of state, where jobs could be found. They might come for holidays, but with Vivien and all staying there, they begged off the past year.

Once Daddy received official notice, Vivien got excited about living in France. Plus, she looked forward to a larger bedroom, even if it meant sharing with Lauren.

Being the youngest of her family, Mama had a special bond with Grandma. Vivien noticed it between Mama and Lauren, too, but she never felt left out. She was Mama's first-born, and Mama often reminded her.

They would be leaving sometime in October. She didn't look forward to the tearful farewell when they all left.

Vivien wondered whether Camp Forrest still existed the same way Camp Breckinridge did. At dinner, Mama mentioned going to see the camp. Grandma said, "It's not there anymore. They tore it all down when the war ended, leaving a big empty field. The people the government stole the land from figured they'd get it back. It never happened. A sort of Air Force center is there now."

"I don't remember," Mama said, looking puzzled.

"I wrote you about it, Lily," Grandma said.

"Hardly seems fair for the government to keep the land. Many of those families farmed there for over a hundred years."

"Can't trust the government," Grandma said.

"I wonder if they'll let us in."

"Prob'ly not. But you can ask."

Vivien lay awake that night, memories coming in pieces of what Mama told her about being born in the hospital at Camp Forrest. If the buildings had all been torn down, the hospital wouldn't be there now. She wondered how many people couldn't visit the hospital they were born in because it no longer existed. She never wanted to see the inside of another hospital for the rest of her life, especially an abandoned military one. However, it did make her a trifle sad, as if a part of her attachment to Manchester had disappeared. It didn't matter she'd been born there a long time ago.

Mama telephoned several officials over the next few days to see if people could get on the base. She explained about her affiliation with Camp Forrest and mentioned her being a military spouse with an ID card. Someone told her she could visit but nothing existed of the old camp. Her time on base would be limited to the headquarters building mostly. She decided to at least drive to the gates of the Air Force base and take a look.

They drove south. The base formed one point of a triangle on the map with Manchester to the northeast, and Tullahoma, more to the southwest, at two other points. Mama packed a lunch, planning to stop at a park she remembered in the vicinity to eat. Being the elder, Vivien got to sit in the front seat on the passenger's side. Once they reached the paved road, she rolled down the window for the air to cool inside and cranked out the small butterfly window to keep the air from blowing directly on her. Mama used the little window to flick the ashes from her cigarettes out of the car and she spotted a trace of ash on the rubber seal. She tried to brush it away, but it wouldn't budge.

Vivien looked forward to the drive and since they couldn't see any of the actual buildings Mama remembered, she felt comfortable with going onto the base. If they could. Soon after they left, Mama began singing "Don't Be Cruel," an Elvis Presley song. Mama and Lauren loved Elvis, but Vivien preferred Pat Boone. She joined in the singing, anyway. "Heart-break Hotel" came next. The three of them knew all the words.

They arrived at the main entrance in twenty-five minutes, after being stuck behind a tractor pulling a wagon piled high with bales of hay. They finally passed it on the two-lane road and made better time.

Mama pulled the Chevy to the side of the road at the entrance and sat a moment looking around. "I don't think this is where the main gate was for Camp Forrest."

They got out of the car and walked to the other side of the road to look across at the imposing new entrance. A large sign on the right side read ARNOLD ENGINEERING DEVELOP-MENT CENTER. Above that, UNITED STATES AIR FORCE.

A couple of cars turned into the drive, the drivers giving them a long look. Another car stopped beside Mama and the driver, wearing an officer's uniform, rolled down his window.

"May I help you?"

"Oh, no," Mama said. "I'm trying to decide if this is where the gate into Camp Forrest stood."

"No, it's long gone. You from around here?"

"I used to be. I live in Manchester right now, waiting for my husband to take us to France later this year."

"He was stationed at Forrest?"

"Yes. Seems like a lifetime ago."

He told her the same thing she'd already learned about

being allowed to enter the headquarters building. She thanked him and he drove in. She stood another minute, then the girls followed her back across the road and got into the car.

For a moment Mama looked like she would cry, but she blew her nose on her handkerchief and smiled. "Well, there goes my plan. I wanted to show you where Vivien was born. The barracks building your father lived in and the PX. We used to go dancing at the club. All gone." She sighed and started the car. "Let's go have our picnic."

"Can we take our picture at the sign there beside the entrance?" Vivien asked. "Daddy might like to see it." The 35 mm camera sat on the seat between them and she picked it up.

"Why not." Mama turned the car off.

She showed Vivien how to operate the camera and got her to take a picture of her and Lauren beside the sign. She took two pictures of the girls on one side of the sign then they separated to stand on each side. Vivien looked down the road at the guardhouse farther down the entry road leading on base. She remembered the entrance to Camp Breckinridge and imagined the one for Camp Forrest probably looked much the same with the small guardhouse.

"Mama, do you have any pictures of the gate before?"

"I think so, but they're packed away in a box."

Vivien started across the road but movement far to the right caught her attention. She looked over toward the sign. Nothing there. She turned in a circle. She had an uneasy feeling, as if someone watched.

Mama and Lauren reached the car, but Vivien stood watching the sign. After a moment, a young girl appeared from behind it. About the same height as Lauren, with black hair falling straight and below her ears. She wore a blue dress with a full skirt. Even at the distance, her eyes looked clear and dark and oddly shaped.

The girl stood looking back at Vivien. Her features appeared well-defined, yet they swirled as if a mist rose and fell between them.

Vivien looked away when Mama called her name.

"Coming." She looked back toward the sign, but the girl had disappeared.

CHAPTER
FIVE

The night air was hot and still. The back bedroom in Grandma's old house got little air circulation even with the window opened all the way to create a draft. Vivien, sticky with sweat from the heat, couldn't sleep. She slipped out of bed, and hoping to not waken Mama or Lauren, made her way barefoot to the back porch.

Clouds covered the moon, leaving the sky sparkling with stars. She never tired of watching them blink and wink. An occasional falling star streaked across the blackness, disappearing so quickly she often wondered if she'd seen it. The straight-back, cane-bottom chair creaked when she sat down. She saw better in the dark than a lot of people and could make out the deeper darkness of the well and smokehouse attached at the back. The grey wood of the barn, a good distance to her right and back near the tree line, looked lighter. The doors stood open like a huge black mouth, open to catch the night bugs.

The clouds moved past the moon. It lit up the garden next to the outhouse, creating twisted shadows. The green cornstalks, nearing maturity, looked like figures of black monsters watching the house. Vivien never saw them like that before on the many nights sitting out on the porch, either alone or with the rest of the family.

Katydids, crickets, and a myriad of other insects provided music for the dance of the fireflies. She watched the points of light flash on and off and remembered the girl at the sign into the Air Force base. She appeared to be Asian. Her expression serious. Or maybe sadness drew the corners of her mouth down. Her sudden appearance and disappearance made Vivien believe the girl was a ghost, or a haint as Grandma would call her.

Why would an Asian girl haunt an Air Force base near Manchester, Tennessee?

She'd hoped to never see another ghost. At least, a ghost of a nurse in an abandoned hospital made some sense. This apparition did not. She had to admit, though, that her curiosity was roused.

Vivien sighed and listened to the night sounds. No breeze freshened the air, but even in the stillness, breathing came easier than inside the house. The noises of insects and tree frogs lulled her into sleepiness. A mosquito bit her arm, and she smacked at it.

Re-awakened, she yawned. Maybe she should spread one of Grandma's old quilts on the porch. Lying on it with a pillow would make it possible to sleep out here. Thinking about the plan came much more easily than getting up and doing it. While she considered moving, a glance at the deeply shadowed well house revealed a rising white mist.

A low, rock wall encircled the deep, dark opening into the earth. A square sheet of metal lay across it to keep things from falling into the water below. The mist oozed through the small gaps between irregular stone and flat metal, drifting up toward the roof. The mist spread across the underside and spilled upward, growing thicker, into the night sky. The air turned cold and she shivered.

Vivien got to her feet and backed toward the screen door. Something rubbed across her ankle. She cried out and jumped back, tripping over the leg of the rocking chair. She braced herself on the arm of the chair to keep from falling and looked down. Grey, Grandma's long-haired, half feral tabby cat, looked up expectantly. She meowed and Vivien shivered and looked toward the well. The mist disappeared.

Grey jumped up on the chair and meowed again. Vivien picked her up, sat down, and set the cat on her lap. Grey purred and rubbed against her chin. The vibrations and warmth of the small body calmed her. The cat, usually feeding a litter of kittens under the porch, let Grandma feed her and occasionally touch her. Only Vivien could pick her up and pet her. The two had an attachment of a sort and it made Vivien feel special. The purring chased away the dread she felt at the sight of the mist.

The urge to pee came over her. She squeezed her legs together and glanced at the outhouse. The idea of going out there in the dark and stepping into the smelly wooden box scared her. Going back into the bedroom and using the chamber pot meant she might wake Mama. She opted for a third choice.

She set Grey on the porch and stepped off onto the grass toward the side of the house with the repaired wall. She pulled down her baby doll pajama bottoms and crouched down, being sure she faced uphill. Finished, she returned to the porch and sat in the chair. Grey jumped back onto her lap while Vivien considered going inside for the quilt and pillow.

Next thing she knew, Mama shook her awake. "Did you sleep out here all night?"

Vivien looked around. "Yes, ma'am." Yellow tinged the sky on the eastern horizon. A few morning birds sang and Grey had disappeared. The air smelled cool and sweet.

"Go on in to bed," Mama said.

Vivien let Mama guide her back to the bed where Lauren slept. Mama covered her with the sheet and kissed her forehead. Grey sneaked in and curled up beside her when Mama left the room.

CHAPTER
SIX

The second time, Vivien woke from a dream and lay quietly thinking about it. It didn't seem like a dream. The longer she lay there, the more it faded.

She sat up and rubbed her eyes. Both Lauren and Grey had left the bed. The cat never slept with her before. Maybe she missed having a litter of kittens to mother and felt lonely. Maybe she'd been scared, too.

Vivien got up and put on a pair of shorts and a halter top. The heat of the day made wearing fewer clothes more comfortable, in spite of Grandma's disapproval. Girls should be better covered, she said. She approved even less of Mama's halter dresses, but she'd stopped expressing her disapproval, simply frowning and shaking her head.

Vivien tiptoed through the kitchen and out the back door, closing the screen door quietly. It all looked normal. No white mist. No black shadowy creatures. Insects buzzed and birds sang. As the day grew hotter, the birds would grow quiet, leaving only the insects to fly about.

What scared her so much last night?

Grey followed her outside and now trotted toward the garden, probably going hunting. Vivien reached to open the screen door. It's Saturday! Shopping day. Grandma did her shopping in town on Saturdays, and the girls would go to the public library and get their week's supply of books. They would all pile into the car about eleven and head down the dirt road, dust rising behind them, to the McMinnville highway, where they'd turn right into town.

She pulled the screen door open as Grandma set breakfast for her and Lauren on the table. Her little sister appeared from the living room. The eggs had been gathered by them yesterday, from wherever the hens laid them. Some laid in the barn, others almost anywhere they could be hidden on the ground.

At night, many of the roosters and hens roosted in a tree, climbing up a board braced against it at a 45-degree angle. Although they were safer from predators there, the tree provided no place to lay their eggs. The bacon came from a neighbor who traded for Grandma's eggs. Milk and butter for the corn bread came from another neighbor.

Sliced white bread appeared in stores a couple of years before, but Grandma wouldn't have any of it. She either baked a loaf or two, or she fixed cornbread or biscuits. Those were fine with the girls, but they also liked when Mama bought the Rainbow white bread for the times the three of them sat down to a meal. They particularly liked it for cinnamon toast, made in the oven.

"Grandma," Vivien said around a mouthful of scrambled egg. "What's in the old smokehouse?" It shared a wall with the back side of the well house. As far as she knew, no one ever went inside.

"Don't talk with your mouth full," Grandma said.

She poured boiling water from the kettle into the metal dishpan sitting in the wide kitchen sink. The house had running cold water from the well, but no hot water. It would cool while the girls ate so they could wash the dishes when they finished eating. Vivien checked the clock on the new electric stove, which replaced the wood cook stove last year.

"Just old furniture. Maybe a few books. I think there's a trunk. It's all junk."

Nothing which might cause a white mist to rise from the well, Vivien guessed. No way would she go in there, no matter what. But her curiosity wouldn't let her not ask.

"What kind of books?"

"I don't remember for sure. Maybe a gazetteer. A couple of old Bibles. Old paperbacks."

"What's a gazetteer?" Lauren asked.

"Oh, has maps and other information about countries."

The girls finished eating and jumped up to gather the dirty dishes. They scraped the dregs into the slop bucket. Vivien washed and Lauren dried. They wiped off the gingham-checked oil cloth covering the table and went into the bedroom to fetch their sandals. The original space, where Vivien, Lauren, and Mama slept, had been built as a one-room cabin many decades before. Grandma didn't remember if she or Papa ever knew the name of the original owner. The newer part of the house consisted of the kitchen, long living room, and Grandma's small bedroom.

The original, square room held two double beds. At the far end stood a huge stone fireplace unused for years. Sometimes it sounded like a bird had gotten trapped in the chimney. The only window looked out onto the front porch, inaccessible from inside. Grandma kept her houseplants out there.

Boxes and a trunk sat in the middle of the room, with their

clothes and a few other personal items. The old trailer house they lived in when posted to Breckinridge sat right next to the house, inside piled with boxes with the rest of their stuff.

They'd brought the trailer with them, thinking they would live in it. Daddy had planned to hook up water and electricity, but it proved too difficult. When he tested the furnace, it wouldn't stay lit no matter what he did. One of the jalousie windows broke in the move and he covered the entire window with cardboard held in place with duct tape. Add to that the difficulty in setting it up evenly on the slope made it easier to move into Grandma's extra bedroom.

Mama and Grandma were already in the car when the girls left the house. They ran to the gravel driveway and climbed into the back of the Chevy. It was hot in the car, but they knew better than to roll down the windows. Dust from the road would cover them all in minutes. Once on the paved highway, all the windows went down.

Vivien waved to her friend Emily standing in front of her parents' little store on the corner when they reached McMinnville Highway. She and her younger sister, Jean, often went down to the ford, a shallow arm of the Little Duck River, to swim with Vivien and Lauren. Sometimes, Vivien took a bar of soap and she and Lauren bathed in the cool water. The last time, Emily also brought a pack of cigarettes she took from the store, and they tried smoking. Each of them coughed and choked, but Emily and Vivien didn't let it stop them. After a time, they each smoked a second cigarette. It got only a bit easier, and they said they liked it. The younger sisters refused the dubious pleasure.

Vivien put her hand out the window and let the wind push against it. They passed a few farms before reaching Manchester city limits. Fields planted with corn and wheat.

Horses in one pasture, cows in another. They passed their church, and Vivien saw Grandma frown. They hadn't been back since the nasty incident of the outside wall of the house.

Manchester was a small farming community, with a population of nearly 3,000. Downtown centered around the courthouse, an imposing two-story, red brick building. A drug store, movie theater, Benjamin Franklin dime store, and other shops occupied the four sides. A small restaurant, the Owl, where Mama worked as a waitress after graduating from high school, sat on one corner.

Sometimes the girls went to a Saturday matinee, either a western movie or a monster movie. The movie theater, the only place in town with air conditioning, had a sign on the marquee, "It's Cool Inside." Going to the pictures on a Saturday gave them a chance to cool off. Mama didn't let them go back since seeing *The Creeping Unknown*, which gave Vivien nightmares for three nights.

They drove through town to the library on Hillsboro Road. "We'll be back at 1:30," Mama called to them while they climbed out. A big clock behind the main desk at the entrance would tell them when they should look for the car.

Large ceiling fans whirred high above them. Pull-down shades covered the windows, lowering both the light and the heat.

Lauren went off to the children's section, and Vivien hurried toward the history shelves. She searched the Tennessee history section for anything on Camp Forrest. She found a thin history of Manchester and two books on Tullahoma. Neither mentioned much about Camp Forrest and instead had sections about the years before the war when Camp Peay occupied the site.

She went to the main desk to see if the librarian could help. Mrs. O'Shea and she became friends over the past few months, and she'd helped locate books on a number of subjects.

"What are you looking for today?" the librarian asked.

"Anything on Camp Forrest if you have it."

"We don't have much. It's probably a bit early for anyone to write a history of the camp. We may have a few magazine articles."

"Anything would be great. My father was stationed there, you know. I was born there, too."

"No, I didn't know. Your daddy served in the Army."

"Yes. We went out there the other day, but there's nothing left."

Mrs. O'Shea led the way to the periodical section. "The poor farmers who owned the land never got it back. But I guess it's good for Tullahoma to have the Air Force move in. Lots of jobs, new people, homes being built."

She thumbed through several magazines. "Ah, here's one." She handed Vivien a copy of a National Geographic. "It's about the wind tunnel the Air Force built there, but it includes a brief history of the Camp."

She continued looking while Vivien opened the journal and looked at the pictures. One was a picture of the front gate of Camp Forrest she wished she could show Mama. Mrs. O'Shea found three more magazines with articles that included a little information about the camp. The magazines couldn't be checked out, so Vivien sat at the table with a small note pad and pencil the librarian lent her. She worked fast, reading and making several notes, so she would have time to select books to take home.

One article mentioned prisoners of war. Not only Germans, as at Camp Breckinridge, but Italians and Japanese, too. But the Japanese weren't soldiers. They were civilians interned as enemy aliens. It brought to mind the girl she saw at the Air

Force base gate. The article said whole families were prisoners there, including children.

The presence of POWs at the camp unnerved her, because of the encounter with Nurse Armstrong's ghost at Camp Breckinridge. She died after giving birth to a daughter. The father was a German POW.

SEVEN

S unday morning, Grandma rousted them all out of bed. "We're goin' to church." She'd said nothing the night before about going. While they sat at the table eating breakfast, she told them a new preacher came to the church a short while back and she wanted to check him out.

She found out from Mrs. Fletcher when they talked on the party line Saturday evening. Her friend attended the Methodist church in town, but word got around about the new, younger, and single Brother Echols. Maybe his coming would change things for the better.

After breakfast, the three of them took turns at the kitchen sink brushing their teeth and splashing water in their faces. They got dressed in their Sunday best and piled into the Chevy. Mama drove a bit slowly so they wouldn't arrive too early.

A few cars sat in the gravel parking lot when they arrived. "The usual early birds," Grandma said. "The blue and white must be the new preacher's."

They got out and walked to the doors, two by two, each with a Bible in hand. The girls carried the new white Bibles they got for Easter. Grandma always carried her old one, so well read the corners were worn away making it look like half of a Moon Pie. Mama's was sort of in between, both in color and age.

Grandma led the way to her usual row and they filed in. More people arrived and there were lots of stares and low whispers. Mrs. Trent came over.

"It's good to see you, Opal Lee. It's been too long."

Grandma nodded, her jaws set tight. She looked beyond her former friend. Mrs. Trent opened her mouth to speak but walked away instead. In a few moments, a family of four approached the row. They stopped and looked at Grandma. She turned and glared at them.

"I guess we can sit over there." The husband steered them to another row. They ended up moving next to the wall when an older family claimed their usual seats nearer the center aisle.

Grandma whispered, "Newcomers."

A crowd filled the pews. Either they approved of the new preacher, or people wanted to check him out, like Grandma. Vivien hadn't seen so many there since Easter, before the incident of Jesus's likeness on the house wall. A steady buzz of low voices filled the room. Catching an occasional word, it seemed Grandma's return caught the congregation's attention. The new pastor took his seat behind the podium and the pianist played a hymn on the piano. They all sat quietly, in supposed contemplation.

The song ended and Brother Echols stepped up behind the podium. "I see new faces amongst us this morning," he said. He nodded toward Grandma. "New to me, at least. Mrs. Flynn, her lovely daughter, and granddaughters have returned to join us in worship."

Mrs. Trent must have told him. She always needed to blow

things up out of proportion. Grandma nodded, thanking the pastor for his kind words.

Vivien couldn't take her eyes off him. He stood several inches taller than Brother Davis. His blond hair, combed back from his face, lay in waves. It seemed all Baptist preachers wore black suits, but Brother Davis's fit perfectly.

He seemed almost too handsome to be a man of God. She wondered if he was married — remembered Grandma said he was single — and scolded herself for thinking of such a thing about a man of God and in church. Married or not, he looked much older than her, just like Walt, the lifeguard at the pool at Camp Breckinridge. Even so, she spent most of her thoughts during the sermon daydreaming about him.

They sang a hymn and Brother Echols said a few words about accepting Jesus as their savior. The call to come forward began for those not yet baptized. Vivien kept her head down, not wanting to move in a way others would take for her intending to walk forward. She wasn't ready to accept Jesus in her heart, unsure what she believed. At the age of twelve, they considered her old enough, but she felt no need to walk to the preacher standing in the front of the dais while everyone sang "Just As I Am."

Movement to her right caught her attention. No one sat in those chairs. She turned to look but saw nothing unusual. Mama patted her leg, reminding her to sit still.

The call ended, a final prayer said, and everyone stood. Mama's watch read twelve noon. Grandma looked at her own watch and nodded approvingly. Brother Echols made his way to the entrance while more music played on the piano, and people streamed out behind him. When Vivien came to the pastor and shook his hand, she felt herself blush. Lauren pushed her from behind. Grandma said something to him, but thanks to Lauren, Vivien couldn't hear it.

The time came when those attending services milled around in the parking lot, catching up on gossip, airing grievances. Vivien wondered if anyone would ask about the hen's blood Jesus. Grandma nodded once or twice to people she knew but didn't stop as usual to gab. She herded them to the car. Mama drove leisurely home, everyone looking forward to a fried chicken dinner, the first since what Grandma referred to as "the incident."

They all changed out of their Sunday best and soon sat down to lunch. The girls did the dishes and cleaned up the kitchen. Mama and Grandma lay down for a nap, leaving the two girls to their own devices. Lauren talked excitedly about Elvis Presley being on the Steve Allen Show later.

Bored, Vivien went out to the front yard and sat on the swing hanging down from a branch of one of the huge walnut trees. She sat with her back to the dirt road, which curved around the property. On that side, the yard ended abruptly in a steep bank down to a narrow ditch between the bank and the road. She didn't like to look down when she swung toward the road.

Even in the shade of the tree, sweat cooled her as it ran down Vivien's back. She swung slowly and the movement of air helped. A car passed on the road, raising a cloud of dust that leaned slightly in the direction of the car's path. She twisted the ropes of the swing to face the road and watched the dust settle.

For the first time, she missed Camp Breckinridge. Playing Canasta with the Moody boys. Running all over the camp, exploring. The pool. She didn't miss the hospital. Well, maybe in the days before Nurse Armstrong's ghost appeared.

She kept occupied during the school year. Playing at recess. Being in class. Homework. Never a free moment. Most of the time, she didn't mind homework. Except math. She wanted to be good at math but couldn't seem to catch on. She didn't fail but earning a "C" hurt her pride. Those darn fractions and division. She'd have to work harder next year.

She'd noticed how grown-ups always asked boys what they wanted to be when they grew up. Most around Manchester would end up as farmers, whether they wanted to or not. The farms were owned and worked by the same families for generations.

Those same grown-ups rarely asked girls what they wanted to be. They assumed girls would grow up to be women who got married, had children, many of them dying young. Her father's mother died early after having eight children in ten years. She'd overhead Mama and Daddy discussing having more children. Mama reminded him about his own mother.

"I don't intend to die before age forty because I had a baby nearly every year," Mama said.

For once, Daddy agreed with her decision, but they knew he wanted a son. Having only a rudimentary understanding of how children were conceived and born, Vivien had no idea how they would prevent it. Having only one sibling worked well for her and she hoped to keep it that way.

Instead of swinging, and already having twisted the ropes, she twisted tighter, then let the ropes untwist, spinning her around. In the middle of untwisting for the third time, she caught a glimpse of a girl walking toward the house on the side road leading north.

Vivien put her foot down to stop spinning and faced the house. She twisted the swing around to face the road, but the road sat empty. She got off the swing and walked toward the edge of the bank. No one in sight, left or right. Five or ten miles north to the next farm. Except for the curve to the right, she could see for a good distance. No sign of the girl. She couldn't have gotten out of her sight so quickly.

She sat on the swing again, trying to remember what the girl looked like. What she wore. The color of her hair? Black. Her face? Nothing but a blur. No better luck with the rest of her appearance. Even so, it must be the same Asian girl.

Vivien shivered. Had she moved from one haunted place to another?

Lauren came from around the house. "Viv, do you want to play pitch?"

She almost said, no. But throwing a baseball back and forth might take her mind off the mysterious girl.

They'd only thrown the ball a couple of times when Emily and her sister arrived, inviting them to go to the ford. "I'll ask Mama," Lauren said. The two of them ran into the house.

They found Mama sitting in the living room with a book. She said they could go and to be careful. They changed into their bathing suits, grabbed a couple of towels, and ran outside, the screen door slamming behind them. They didn't bother taking a bar of soap because they took their baths in the washtub Saturday night.

The four girls walked down the dirt road, all wearing the new flip flops they discovered recently. They cost little and made great sandals for summer. Made of rubber, they could be worn in the water and would dry out quickly. The riverbed of the ford consisted of rocks which hurt if they walked on them in their bare feet.

Once they were out of sight of the house, Emily pulled a pack of L&M cigarettes from the pocket of the shirt she wore over her bathing suit.

"Oh, good," Vivien said.

She turned and looked at Lauren who shook her head. Vivien shrugged. She didn't have to smoke if she didn't want to.

A quarter of a mile down the road, they turned left down a

narrow track. They'd never seen any sort of car drive down it, and the weeds grew tall this time of year. The track had been so well used in the past, it would be many more years before it became totally overgrown. The sweet smell of honeysuckle filled her nostrils. Vivien often saw deer tracks along it, so animals would help keep it clear. Daddy said the two deep ruts along its length were made by horse-drawn wagons.

They reached the river's edge. Walking so far had gotten them all hot and sweaty in spite of the shade from trees overhanging the track, and they looked forward to the coolness of the water.

The track continued up the other bank, disappearing into the woods. Vivien always wondered how far it went and what hid in those woods.

They hung the towels on tree branches and jumped into the water. In the deepest part, it came to Vivien's waist. Emily was a little taller while the level of water for Lauren and Jean came up to their chests.

They all knew how to swim, but Vivien and Lauren had only swum in a pool before moving to Manchester. Here, no wall to kick off of, and the pressure when putting your head under water felt different.

They waded around, enjoying the coolness, dunking themselves to wet their whole bodies. They splashed around and each other. Vivien changed to the backstroke. She pulled the goggles Mama got her for swimming in the river down over her eyes and rolled over onto her stomach. She dove under the water and touched the rocks, unable to see much in the murky water.

She surfaced for a gulp of air and dove again. She swam one way, turned and swam back. A face appeared below her, and she stared into a pair of dark eyes. Something wrapped around her lower leg and she tried to scream. She choked on the water and struggled to stand. When she got her feet under her, she couldn't stop coughing. Emily patted her on the back.

"Are you all right?" Emily asked

Vivien tugged on the goggles to get them off. She nodded, unable to speak and climbed out of the water. For several minutes, she bent over trying to catch her breath. "Which one of you did that?"

"Did what?" Emily asked.

"Grabbed my leg." She didn't want to say anything about the face nose to nose with her.

"We weren't anywhere near you," Emily said. The two younger sisters nodded.

"Something did."

"Probably a weed," Emily said.

After more protests of innocence, she had to accept none of them grabbed her leg. They spread out the towels on the ground, and Emily brought out the pack of cigarettes.

The air dried them while they sat, telling stories and sharing their dreams. Vivien and Emily talked about boys in their class they liked or didn't like and crushes on actors in TV shows.

"I like Elvis," Lauren piped up.

"Oh, yuck," Vivien said.

Vivien stole the occasional glance at the river for any sign of whatever grabbed her. Mama warned them to watch out for snakes in the water. Vivien didn't intend to run home and tell what happened. If she did, Mama and Grandma would never let them come to the ford again.

CHAPTER
EIGHT

S unday night they all gathered in the living room to watch the Steve Allen Show. Elvis came on last. Mama and Lauren sat spellbound. Grandma crocheted. Vivien groused about all the girls screaming in the audience so you couldn't even hear him sing. It distracted her from what happened at the ford. When she went to bed, however, the image of the girl's face kept her awake.

Vivien slept badly for nearly a week, either unable to fall asleep or waking from dreams of being under water. Mama blamed it on her watching another monster picture on late night TV.

"No more scary movies for you," she said. Vivien groaned inwardly, not wanting to tell Mama she might be seeing ghosts again.

But she liked watching those movies, and her nightmares didn't come from them. At least, not now. Several nights, when she floated near sleep, the face came to her. Unnaturally white with black eyes. She sensed from the shape of the eyes and the coal black hair, the girl was not white. Not black, either. She looked a little like the girl who waited on tables at the Chinese restaurant in town.

Once Mama took all of them to eat there one Saturday after shopping. The girl fascinated her, no bigger than Lauren, yet old enough to wait on tables. Both she and Lauren stood slightly taller than most other kids their ages, which made the girl seem smaller. Her skin color puzzled Vivien.

"All orientals are called yellow," Mama said. "They aren't quite that color."

"They're smaller than us Americans?"

"Sometimes."

After seeing the girl in the water, Vivien compared her to the girl she saw walking along the road toward the house. She hadn't seen her clearly either time, except for the hair, the same dark color. Maybe.

A few days after the scare at the ford, Vivien asked Grandma if she could look through the stuff in the smokehouse. Boredom set in as it often did during the summer. Except last summer, which she preferred to think of only in terms of the pool and Walt. She wanted to forget the hospital, Nurse Armstrong, and the POW cemetery.

Grandma said she could look around, "but be careful." Things had been thrown inside higgledy-piggledy and there might be danger of stacks falling over on top of her. Vivien asked if she could take the oil lantern they used outside at night, but Grandma said, no. "If it falls over, the whole place might burn down."

They scrounged up a couple of flashlights, one needing new batteries. With both flashlights finally working, Vivien approached the door of the smokehouse. No one set foot inside in ages. Grandma said the building was full of stuff when they bought the place. She didn't know how long it had been since anyone used the building as a smokehouse, but never in her experience.

The hinges creaked on the door made of old, grey, iron-hard boards, heavy and solid. Vivien stepped up. First thing, she needed to prop the door open. She found a large piece of firewood and set it against the bottom of the door. Dust rose when she stepped inside and with each step she took. The wood floor felt solid, but it creaked in places. She placed one of the flashlights right inside the door so she could find it easily if the other stopped working.

A narrow path between piles of debris led inward and turning to the right toward the back. Sunlight shone through gaps between the warped boards of the wall, lighting thin strips on the floor and on the piles, giving the space a twilight glow. She needed the flashlight to see any details. The dust made her cough. Maybe she should tie a scarf around her nose and mouth.

The flashlight shone on bits of chairs and other pieces of furniture. Most appeared broken and tossed in there instead of repairing or discarding. No orderly stacking. A chair back here, legs there. Many mystery pieces whose function couldn't be guessed at.

She took a few more steps inside. Cut firewood formed the base of the pile right inside the door, probably to be used in smoking meat or maybe for Grandma's old wood cookstove. Pieces of board, grey with age, sat stacked on top. No way could she divide it all into individual piles.

She moved toward the turn in the path. Her blouse got caught on the leg of a stool and she stepped back to get it loose. Movement above caught her eye, and she gasped. Iron hooks swung slightly from the ceiling. The vibrations of her walking must have disturbed them. She exhaled loudly and chided herself for being so easily spooked.

The turn in the path led to more overlapping piles of junk. They stood a little higher than just inside the door, wood and metal junk reaching almost to the ceiling. Grandma mentioned books, but she couldn't see any.

Part of an old rocking horse caught her eye. A rocker was missing from the bottom and part of the yarn mane. The eye on the side she could see was missing. On the other side of the path, the seat, one arm, and one rocker of a rocking chair sat upside down on the top.

Vivien coughed again and the door slammed shut. She spun around and the flashlight flickered but stayed on. At least she wouldn't have to get the other one. She walked toward the door, but something moved to her right. She stopped and held her breath, searching for whatever caught her attention. A little below eye level, what looked like a scrapbook lay under a small wooden box. Above, a deep pile of more wood and old quilts.

She went to the door, opened it, and propped the piece of wood against it again. Better this time she hoped.

Walking back down the path, she couldn't find the scrapbook. She went toward the back wall and turned. She could only see it from that direction. One tug proved that pulling it out from the middle would bring the whole thing tumbling down on top of her. She needed a way to prop up the pile, but it stood too high for her to even reach the top.

The pile rocked and creaked when she tugged at it again. If it could be steadied, it might be possible to pull the scrapbook loose. She would need help. She ran outside and called for Lauren. When she found her little sister, Vivien told her what she needed. Lauren didn't want to go into the smokehouse.

"It's dark and dirty and smells." She'd never been inside, of course.

"It's not so bad. It will only take a couple of minutes."

"You sure?"

Vivien nodded with all the enthusiasm she could muster. Lauren reluctantly agreed. Vivien grabbed a straight back chair with a wood seat from the porch and they carried it into the smokehouse. For a moment Vivien considered who should hold up the pile and who should pull out the scrapbook. She stood taller and could lean against more of the pile. She was also stronger and would have better luck pulling out the scrapbook.

"Well?" Lauren said.

"Okay. I'm taller and when I'm up on the chair, I'll lean against the stack while you pull out the scrapbook. You'll have to do it slowly, a little at a time. Maybe work it back and forth."

Lauren bit her lip and nodded. Vivien climbed up on the chair and raised her arms and stretched to reach the top of the stack. She leaned her whole weight against it and felt a bit of a shift. It settled and she felt stable.

"Okay. Start pulling."

Lauren pulled and twisted the scrapbook. Vivien felt every little movement of the stack. "I got it," Lauren cried out.

The stack began to crumble. Vivien pressed harder against the tangle of wood and metal, but without enough strength, it collapsed. She and Lauren both screamed. Vivien tumbled from the chair, landing on her stomach on the floor. A few pieces of wood fell onto her. She lay stunned, coughing on dust and blinking to clear her eyes.

"Vivien," Lauren called softly from the doorway. "Are you all right?"

"What's going on?" Mama's voice demanded.

Vivien groaned. She'd hoped neither Mama nor Grandma heard the noise. No such luck.

"Nothing," she called out.

"Nothing? Look at this mess."

Mama lifted the pieces off of her elder daughter. She raised her to her feet and took hold of her shoulders. Vivien felt shaken but tried to act like nothing serious happened. Mama looked her up and down. "You seem to be in one piece."

"We'll clean it up," Vivien said. She looked toward the door for her little sister, but Lauren had gone.

Clearing the aisle of fallen pieces by herself turned out to be impossible. The pile was too tangled, the things too heavy. The original stack stood too high to lift anything to the top. Mama told her to forget it and come outside.

"It should all be burned," she said.

Vivien carried the chair she'd stood on to the porch and went back inside for one more item: the wooden box that fell to the floor. She carried it to the porch and set it on a chair. Before looking through the box, she went into the kitchen and rinsed dust off her face and hands. She felt like she needed a bath, but she'd have to wait until Saturday. Maybe she could wash off better before bedtime.

Time to find Lauren and the scrapbook. Her little sister sat in the swing practicing omphaloskepsis. Vivien had heard a teacher use the word to describe a fellow teacher and looked it up in the unabridged dictionary in the classroom. It took several tries at the spelling. The word meant "contemplating one's navel." Vivien took it to mean a person shirking their job.

She walked up to her sister. "Where's the scrapbook?"

Lauren pointed to the front porch. "Are you all right?" Vivien nodded. "Did Mama punish you?"

"No." If she was punished, then Mama would probably punish Lauren, too. "We're okay."

"Good."

Lauren continued swinging while Vivien went to the porch. The scrapbook lay near the huge potted elephant ears. She carried the scrapbook to the back porch, setting it on top of the wooden box. She dusted off both with an old dust cloth she fetched from the house.

She opened the scrapbook first and flipped through the pages, holding the edges. Newspaper clippings once glued to the pages, remained barely attached. The first ones, dated 1942, reported on the arrival of Japanese civilian prisoners of war at Camp Forrest. The reporters called them "enemies of America living within our borders." Several pictures showed whole families, women, men, and small children, being herded off trains. Others showed them passing wire gates framed with wood. They carried few personal possessions, mostly a suitcase or two, and dressed in what seemed like nice clothes. Guards in uniforms and holding rifles watched them file by.

Why did the government consider them enemies? The article said they were American citizens who lived in California. None of them seemed to have done anything bad.

After the first few pages, Vivien sat back in the chair. Daddy served at Camp Forrest in 1942. He and Mama met that year and got married in 1943. She couldn't remember when they moved to Camp Carson in Colorado. Had he been one of the soldiers guarding these Japanese prisoners?

She'd seen war movies and knew Japanese soldiers did terrible things. Daddy said things about them when the movies came on late night TV, until Mama scolded him for using such words in front of his daughters. He served some-where in Europe and never faced the so-called Nips.

She turned to the back of the scrapbook. The last two pages were empty. The final article reported the death of several Japanese, men and women, killed while working outside the camp. The men worked on farms and in the feed store in Manchester. The women worked in the pajama factory in Tullahoma, then making uniforms for American soldiers. Tullahoma sat closer to the camp, and more of the prisoners worked there. Reading the headlines frightened her and she skipped over the details of the stories.

Over several months, many of the prisoners, both soldiers and civilians, died. "Under suspicious circumstances." The police and courts explained the deaths away as accidents or suicides and it looked as if they arrested no one. The same had been true with the German POWs at Camp Breckinridge. It didn't seem right to her, but maybe she didn't have the whole picture.

She set aside the scrapbook without reading all the articles. The stories upset her, and she didn't want to read anymore. The wooden box might be more interesting.

Writing on the lid of the box read, "El Producto" in big letters. In smaller letters underneath, "Altas." Inside the lid, an advertisement for the cigars featured a lady dressed elegantly in a red dress with the word "Altas" repeated in one corner. The box felt heavy, but because of the contents, not the box itself, which was made of balsa or a similar light wood. She opened the box. Inside lay a lock of black hair, tied with blue ribbon. Vivien took it out and laid it on the scrapbook. Next, a piece of cloth and small trinkets. A few prizes from Cracker Jacks. Under it all, a black and white photo of a young girl. Taken from a distance, too small to see her face clearly.

An Asian girl. With all the articles in the scrapbook, she

must be Japanese. Her dress looked like one Vivien would wear to school. The woods behind her looked familiar. Vivien looked up, then held up the picture. The woods behind Grandma's house looked like the ones in the picture. Such woods would be found almost anywhere, but since whoever took the picture probably lived on the farm, the woods were probably the same.

Out of the corner of her eye, she saw a figure step up onto the porch. She glanced over, thinking it must be a stranger, but no one stood there, or approached the screen door. She looked around. No one in sight. These visions of someone there, but not there, spooked her. They made her both afraid and angry.

"If you want to tell me something, tell me," she said.

No one spoke. Vivien dropped the picture into the box and scooped the other things on top of it. She closed the lid and took the box and the album into the bedroom. She slid them under the bed. Out of sight, out of mind.

CHAPTER

TEN

Vivien led the way up the steps onto the city bus. Mama dropped change into the square box next to the driver. Only one empty seat in the front part of the bus. Lots of empty seats in the back, but a sign said, "Colored Seating." Mama headed to the back and sat down.

"Mama, the sign says these seats are for coloreds," Vivien said.

"It's all right," Mama said. "Sit down." She patted the seat next to her.

Vivien feared colored folks would holler at them for taking their seats. She sat on one side of Mama and Lauren on the other. No one paid them any attention, and they got to their destination with no trouble.

They'd ridden on a Greyhound bus from Manchester to Nashville early so they could get their passport. They needed it to go overseas. They would have come days ago, but Mama didn't have a copy of her birth certificate and a photostatic copy from the Coffee County Clerk's office took several trips and phone calls and a couple of weeks.

Vivien couldn't be sure what a passport meant, except needing one made their moving overseas more real. They were almost ready to move to France. She also learned, much to her chagrin, they must take a series of shots to protect them from several different diseases. To get those, they needed to go to Smyrna Air Force Base, the nearest place to Manchester with a military clinic.

Today, they headed for the main post office in Nashville to fill out an application and have their picture taken. Vivien felt a little disappointed they didn't each have their own passport, instead having one with a picture of the three of them. The clerk told them the passport would be mailed to them in about three weeks, three months before they should be leaving.

They left the post office and Mama led them to a café across the street where they ate lunch. Mama had a salad plate and the girls had sandwiches, and milk shakes for all, a special treat. They walked back to the Greyhound station, checking out store windows along the way. Vivien pointed to dresses and shoes she would love to have, but they were all for grown women.

Vivien fell asleep on the bus back to Manchester, the buzz of muted voices in her ears. She dreamt of a pretty, young Japanese girl. The girl said her name, but Vivien didn't understand it. The girl spoke for several minutes, but either her accent or the soft tone of her voice made it difficult to hear what she said. She seemed to be pleading, but about what? When the bus pulled into the station in Manchester, and she woke, she felt like the girl didn't want her to move away from Manchester.

Grandma picked them up in her old Ford. All the way home, Vivien wondered about the girl in the dream and in the black and white picture. One thing she felt sure of. The two were the same.

ELEVEN

Next morning after breakfast, Vivien pulled the scrapbook and the box from under her bed. She sat on the back porch and put the items on the chair next to her. First, she read each article from the beginning. She learned more about the prisoners, both military and civilian, many of them loaned out to work on farms in the county and businesses in both Tullahoma and Manchester.

With most of the able-bodied men away in the military services, farmers and townspeople needed the help. Even so, not everyone welcomed the presence of the prisoners. Anger at the civilian Japanese had been the worst. Beatings of both women and men occurred, most never reported and no arrests were made. She got most of that information from notes written on the pages of the scrapbook or on the articles, written in a shaky handwriting.

The identity of the person who saved the articles remained a mystery. She suspected the man who owned the farm before Grandpa bought it. The penmanship and spelling left a lot to be desired. A few notes were written in pencil with the point so blunt the words blurred.

About three-quarters of the way through, she came upon an article with a headline, all in capital letters: JAPANESE STUDENT MURDERED.

The victim, a young girl, a student at New Union Elementary School, drowned in the ford. Her father did farm work for Mr. Joseph McCarthy, local farmer and widower.

The girl, aged 13, was found by her father, who searched for her after she didn't come home. He received permission to send her to the New Union Elementary School while he worked during the day on Carl McCarthy's farm. The two lived at the farm instead of Camp Forrest. Local police suspect foul play. They have no suspects as of this writing.

Vivien shivered. She now felt she knew why she saw the face of the young Japanese girl in the river. She searched for her name. She found it a few lines down: Yoshi Narita.

She closed the scrapbook and exchanged it for the wooden cigar box. The black and white photo lay on top, although she remembered — or thought she did — placing it on the bottom. She turned it over. On the back someone wrote the girl's name: Yoshi Narita. She looked from the picture to the lock of black hair. It must be hers.

She'd touched the hair of a dead girl. The realization made her shiver. If this scrapbook and box belonged to Mr. McCarthy, why did he keep the memento?

The writer of the last article she read hinted at something about men and young girls. Vivien sighed. To understand would require her asking Mama what it meant. She'd wanted to keep all of this to herself. Not for any reason she could express, except perhaps Mama would be upset about another ghost appearing to her. This time it scared Vivien because she knew what could happen. The first time, when she met Nurse Armstrong, she had no idea.

She wanted to know what the implication about men and girls meant and agonized over whether to ask. The ghostly encounter at Camp Breckinridge upset Mama. Vivien kept most of what happened to herself, yet she felt Mama understood. Maybe she'd even experienced similar things when younger.

The screen door squeaked open and Mama came out onto the porch with the dishpan. She threw the water into the yard and turned to go back inside.

"Mama."

She started. "Oh, I didn't see you sitting there."

"Sorry. I need to ask you a question."

"What is it?" Mama came over and sat down.

"I got this scrapbook out of the smokehouse." Mama nodded. "And the box, too." Mama looked down at it. "I didn't see the box before," she said. Vivien touched the top of it on the chair between them. "The scrapbook is full of articles about the prisoners of war at Camp Forrest. A lot of them went out to work for farmers." She opened the scrapbook to the story about the girl being found. "Here in this article," she put her index finger on the paragraph, "I don't understand."

"What does it say?" Mama asked.

"Things about men and young girls." Vivien held the scrapbook out to Mama, who set the dishpan down on the porch. She took the book, laying it in her lap and read.

Vivien watched her, noticing frown wrinkles appear between her eyebrows. Mama stopped reading, but she didn't look up for a long moment.

"It has to do with sex doesn't it?" Last year, Mama told her how babies were made, when Vivien had her first menstrual period. She described it as a beautiful experience between two people who loved each other, but what the article hinted at didn't sound beautiful.

Finally, Mama looked at her. "Remember when I told you about not talking to strangers, because some people are bad people, but it's hard to tell who's bad and who isn't?" Vivien nodded. "This is about one kind of bad person. Grown men who love young girls in the same way most men love their wives. It's a sickness. According to this article, the police believed a man sick in that way killed this young girl."

Vivien's face grew hot. "Oh," she said. She didn't completely understand.

"Are you sure you want to read about this?" Mama asked.

"I don't know."

"Has anything else happened? Have you seen ghosts?"

Vivien nodded. "This girl."

"I would prefer you didn't get involved again, especially after what happened the last time."

"I know."

Mama patted her thigh. "Your grandma and I are here if you need us, but we can't interfere. We don't know what you're going through or seeing. We both had similar experiences at about your age but nothing strong like what happens to you. It stopped after we got older."

"I'll be careful."

"Promise you won't let this get you into trouble like the last one."

"I promise."

Mama picked up the dishpan and went back inside. Vivien remembered being frightened with the threats of the ghost of Nurse Armstrong back in Breckinridge. She'd hoped nothing similar would happen again. But this sort of thing ran in their family, handed down from mother to daughter. She remembered a story she read once about a witch. She also inherited it from her mother.

But she couldn't stop thinking about the girl who seemed to plead for her help. What did she expect Vivien to do?

CHAPTER
TWELVE

Vivien closed the scrapbook. She'd finished all of the articles about Yoshi. The story disturbed her, but she didn't understand a lot of what she'd learned even after talking with Mama.

Mr. McCarthy was tried and convicted of murdering Yoshi Narita, in spite of Mr. Narita's protests. For whatever reason, he'd been convinced the farmer didn't kill his daughter. He protested to the police, but they ignored him. They didn't allow him to testify in court at the trial because of who and what he was.

In spite of the police saying there were no suspects right after Yoshi died, Vivien sensed they suspected Mr. McCarthy from the beginning. Reading the testimony at the trial, she learned that right after the Naritas first came to the farm, Yoshi got her hair cut. It had gotten long over the months of intern-ment. With the temper in the community toward the Japanese, Mr. McCarthy took her himself. He must have gotten the lock of hair then, gathered together by the beautician, whom he paid extra. The beautician apparently was reluctant, but the extra money persuaded her.

It appeared the picture of Yoshi was taken right after they got back to the farm. Vivien took the picture out of the box. Yes, the girl wore short hair and appeared to be in her best dress.

Why would the community want to blame Mr. McCarthy for her death? It couldn't be because he hired Mr. Narita to work on the farm. They helped out on lots of farms in spite of the general hatred toward them. The farmers considered them hard workers. She needed to find out more about Mr. McCarthy. But how?

A lot of people now living in Manchester must have known him but would anyone still living in town want to talk about what happened? She'd learned when trying to find information in Morganfield, the nearest town to Camp Breckinridge, that people could be very testy about the past.

Did she dare ask Mrs. O'Shea about Mr. McCarthy? She liked the librarian but had no idea how long she'd lived in Manchester. She hoped she could help.

None of the articles said what happened after Mr. McCarthy's trial. Obviously, he sold or lost the farm. Maybe he went to prison. Maybe they executed him. If neither of those things happened, he must have left town. He might still be alive.

The following Saturday, she went to the library as usual. It took a while to screw up her courage and approach Mrs. O'Shea.

"Why do you want to know about Mr. McCarthy?"

"He owned the farm my grandfather bought."

"How do you know?" The librarian appeared more curious about how Vivien knew about the farm.

"The old smokehouse is full of junk. I found an old scrapbook with . . ." She started to say a scrapbook filled with newspaper articles but hesitated. Maybe, at first, she shouldn't mention she had read about the Japanese girl and Mr. McCarthy's trial. She finished, "with papers about the farm."

Mrs. O'Shea stared at her a moment, then down at her hands on the desk. "Have you tried the county clerk's office? I'm sure they have copies or records of deeds and other documents."

"I want to know where he went," Vivien said. "Did he die or did he sell the farm? Does he live around here?" Vivien waited a moment for a response. "Did you know him?"

Mrs. O'Shea's shook her head. "I've lived here since 1947," she said. "I never heard of him or what may have happened to him."

Vivien thought that the librarian was from Manchester and learning she wasn't surprised her. "Where did you come from?" she asked.

"Murfreesboro. I went to college there and thought I'd become a teacher. But this position came open just after I graduated and here I am." She'd been leaning on the counter and now straightened. "I'll see if I can find out anything on your Mr. McCarthy. Your best bet will be the county clerk, or maybe the newspaper."

"Thanks."

Vivien went back to the table to sit with Lauren. Her sister, so involved in the book in front of her, hardly knew she'd been gone. Vivien looked at the title: *Mysterious Island* by Jules Verne. They might be different in so many ways, but they both enjoyed many of the same books.

She took out the notepad she'd bought at the dime store earlier. Actually, she'd gotten a sales book to use. She could write a note and make a carbon copy at the same time. Either the original or the copy could be torn out, and the other left in the book. It would be helpful to have a second copy in case she lost one.

She opened a book from the pile she'd already gathered to read, but she couldn't concentrate. Mrs. O'Shea was right about where to find information. She'd already found loads of information in the newspaper articles. She needed to get to the morgue at the newspaper office. Most newspapers stored copies of back issues on their premises. Too far to walk from the library to the *Manchester Times* office downtown. She could hitchhike like her cousin Johnny did, but Mama would be furious. She didn't want to wait until next Saturday, but she might have to.

As for the county clerk, she wasn't sure what they might know. Grandma would know at least some of the information. She kept up with all the gossip in Manchester and the county. But Vivien didn't want to tell her why she wanted to know. Unless Mama told her about the ghost already. Would she be willing to talk about Mr. McCarthy? Had she known him? The way she talked, Grandpa did all the business. He bought the farm and moved them without a by-your-leave, as she put it. Come to think of it, she had no idea where they lived before then.

Surely, the whole town would have talked about the killing of the young girl and the trial. Such events in a small town must be common gossip. And it didn't happen so long ago.

Vivien made up her mind to visit the newspaper office before asking anyone else for information. If she couldn't find anything there, she would have to decide if asking Grandma was worth the trouble.

CHAPTER
THIRTEEN

Mama agreed to take Vivien to town so she could visit the newspaper office. She couldn't take her until Monday or Tuesday of the next week. She considered it would be better than asking Grandma what she might remember of the affair. Vivien also wanted to buy a better writing tablet. She'd found the sales slips too small. However, Mama found a small pad among her things for writing letters and gave it to her.

Instead of watching TV at night, she sat at the kitchen table and made notes from the scrapbook. She made two separate lists: One included what she'd considered important from the articles. The second, a list of questions, either to find in the newspaper morgue, or to ask Grandma if it was the only way to have them answered. She hoped she wouldn't have to.

The four of them went to church Sunday. The doors stood open along with a couple of the windows for a cross draft. With little air movement, in spite of the open doors, the temperature and humidity left them wiping their brows and fanning themselves with the rigid paper fans attached to a flat stick like a tongue depressor the doctor used.

They took their usual seats. Vivien saw several people look at her and whisper to whomever sat beside them. Mrs. Trent looked her way for a particularly long time. Vivien remembered how people acted over the figure of Jesus on Grandma's wall. But that situation resolved itself, so it couldn't be that.

Did they hear about what she asked Mrs. O'Shea? Nothing else happened to pique their interest in her or her family, had it? If so, Mrs. O'Shea must have told someone, who told someone else.

Pastor Echols rose from the chair behind the podium. He placed his well-worn Bible on the slanted top and bade them all rise. A lot of fly swatting accompanied the singing during the first hymn. Notices and requests for prayers came next and Vivien got lost in the sound of his voice. She fantasized about him and swatted at flies. They would have dinner in a dimly lit café while a waiter played romantic music on a violin, just like in the movies. It didn't seem strange she hadn't thought about him since the last time they came to church.

In between times, she'd daydreamed about David Niven, the suave British actor, Eddie Fisher, a popular singer with a great voice, and even Elvis. She might not like him on general principles, but she couldn't deny he was cute.

Vivien realized she'd been daydreaming when a fly settled on her hand. She sat up straight, no clue to the subject of the sermon. Grandma might ask her thoughts later. Both she and Mama let her know how important it would be for her to accept Jesus as her savior every time they went to Sunday services. Making them happy seemed the only reason to walk to the altar.

She concentrated on the words from the pulpit until she saw movement against the wall to the right. In the space between the rows of pews and the wall a pale figure walked toward the dais. Yoshi stared at the pastor. Vivien put her feet together on the floor, ready to spring forward. One glance around showed no one else saw the apparition. She settled back and watched.

The ghost walked to the dais and stepped up onto it. Slowly she approached the podium. She reached the pastor and stood beside him. She turned slowly, her shoulder pressing against his waist, and rose up on tiptoes to look toward the Bible. Her mouth puckered and she blew. The pages of the Bible fluttered over to another page.

Pastor Echols's hand never moved from the book. Yoshi cocked her head and looked up at him, waiting for him to notice. He smiled and looked down at the page.

"It seems the Lord has chosen another passage," he said with a slight laugh. "He's chosen Genesis 23:4. 'I am a stranger and an alien residing among you; give me property among you for a burying place, so that I may bury my dead out of my sight.'"

He looked puzzled and people in the congregation muttered. It did seem a strange choice, given his original passage posted on the program board. Yoshi looked at Vivien as if to see if she understood. Vivien felt frozen in place, unable to even nod to the girl.

Pastor Echols continued like nothing odd happened. Vivien didn't listen, didn't know if he returned to his original message or if he spoke on the verse Yoshi chose. The ghost stepped down from the dais while he spoke and walked back the way she came. She drew near and Vivien saw her wet hair and clothes. Water ran down her face, dripping from her chin. She stared at Vivien in passing and faded from sight.

Mama patted her leg again. "Turn around," she said. Vivien felt her heart beating and turned back to face the altar.

Soon, they sang the final hymn, "Just As I Am," the anthem for those unbaptized to come forward and accept Jesus. The song ended and Mama sighed. Once again, Vivien almost walked forward to please Mama and Grandma, but couldn't bring herself to do it, knowing she didn't feel the call, the need to be saved. Today, however, she'd been more distracted than usual.

The song ended, Pastor Echols said the blessing, and everyone filed toward the door. He stood outside, shaking hands, thanking people for coming. He looked slightly off-kilter, as if he didn't understand what happened.

He smiled broadly at Vivien and took her hand in his. "Maybe next time, Miss Vivien." She nodded and walked on, her head bowed.

They neared the car when Mrs. Trent and Mrs. Howard called out to Grandma.

The two ladies approached Grandma. "This is your doin', Opal Lee Flynn."

"What's my doin'?"

"You know very well. Something happened there in the church. The pastor, his Bible . . ."

"I have no idea what you're talking about," Grandma said. Vivien could see the color rise in Grandma's face.

Mrs. Trent stepped closer to Grandma. "What is going on? What are you and that granddaughter of yours up to? Always stirring up trouble. Mrs. O'Shea said . . ." Her voice rose and several people stopped on the way to their cars and looked over.

Pastor Echols approached, interrupting Mrs. Trent. "Ladies. Ladies."

"They're up to no good," Mrs. Trent said.

Grandma turned and got into the Chevy. The others followed. Vivien got a mean look from Mrs. Trent.

"How strange," Grandma said.

Mama drove toward home. No one responded. Vivien wondered about the silence of the congregation after the pastor read the verse from Genesis. Why did he read it out? It didn't relate to the posted subject of his sermon. How did he know which verse should be read? She thought back. His hand rested on the Bible when the pages turned.

He never raised his hand to rest it on the new page. He must have believed his hand still rested on the verse he'd selected. When Yoshi walked away and vanished, Vivien felt like her own body deflated like a balloon.

Grandma fussed all the way home. What was wrong with the pastor? Why did Mrs. Trent seem to think she had anything to do with what happened? And what happened anyway? No one responded since she hardly paused for breath.

Mama steered the car into the driveway and the girls piled out. They ran to the bedroom to pull off their Sunday best and get back into shorts and cooler tops.

"Did you see anything?" Lauren asked.

"When?"

"When the preacher read the wrong verse."

"No, why?"

"The way you looked. Did you see a ghost?"

Vivien turned on her little sister. "Don't ever say that again."

Lauren looked startled. "I know you see ghosts. I hoped you wouldn't see any more after what happened at Camp Breckinridge."

"So did I," Vivien said. She stomped out of the bedroom, passing Mama coming in to change.

"What was that all about?" she heard Mama ask behind her. She didn't hear Lauren's response.

Grandma had gotten over her shyness about having chicken for Sunday dinner. The four of them ate fried chicken, mashed potatoes, fresh peas, and peach cobbler until nearly comatose. Vivien took her book out to the back porch and sat in her favorite cane bottom chair. With nothing on TV she wanted to watch, Lauren sat on the swing, pushing herself back and forth lazily. Mama and Grandma settled onto their respective beds for a nap, each with an electric fan blowing on them.

"Hello," a voice called from the front yard. Vivien got up to see who. Emily and her sister appeared around the side of the house.

"Hi," Vivien said, waiting for them to reach the steps to the porch. "What's up?"

"Would you and Lauren like to go for a swim?" Emily surreptitiously pulled a pack of L&Ms from her pocket and shoved them back down.

Vivien hesitated. After the last time, she'd lost her enthusiasm for the ford. But the unbearable heat and humidity made a swim sound too good to pass up.

Mama, half asleep told them, "Go ahead. Be careful."

They promised and changed into their swimsuits. Soon, the four girls strode down the road, laughing and talking. Once they moved out of sight of the house, Emily and Vivien each lit a cigarette, coughing with each puff.

They reached the river and hung the towels on the tree limbs. Vivien stood on the bank for several minutes watching the others frolicking in the water. She stepped in, vowing not to swim under the water or put her face into it.

CHAPTER
FOURTEEN

Mama couldn't take Vivien into town until Tuesday. She needed to pick up a bag of lime for the outhouse and it was convenient to drop Vivien off at the newspaper office on the way to the feed store. They'd arranged to meet at the soda fountain on the square when they'd finished.

A bell over the door rang when Vivien walked in. The newspaper office resembled a regular store with a glass front. She stood just inside the door and looked around. No one came to see what she wanted. A call bell sat on the counter and she tapped it with the palm of her hand. The door on the other side opened and a man came out.

"Hi, there. What can I do for you?"

He looked young, but his hair had gone grey. He wore a white shirt, sleeves rolled up, and a string tie. He smiled warmly.

"Are you the editor?"

He nodded. "Caleb Logan, at your service."

"I'd like to look through old newspapers in your morgue,

please."

The man looked around, frowning slightly. "Everyone's out at the moment. I'm not sure . . . Can you wait?"

Vivien put on her sad face. "My mama dropped me off and I have to meet her when I'm done. I don't think it will take long."

He smiled again. "Sure." He went to the swinging gate and pulled it open. "Come on through."

She followed him down a long hall to a room at the end with no windows, making it dark like in a basement. The single light bulb overhead shone just bright enough to reveal a thin layer of dust on the top of a library table.

"What year are you looking for?"

"1942."

"The whole year?"

She hoped to find the information quickly but decided to ask for a four-month stretch. The articles in the scrapbook appeared in the newspapers daily, from the day they found Yoshi until the end of the trial. She not only wanted to see if Mr. McCarthy's scrapbook lacked any articles, she also wanted to see what else went on during the same time.

Mr. Logan pulled a large binder from a shelf about shoulder high to Vivien and set it on the table. "We have one binder to each month, roughly four weeks," he explained. "This is the shelf for 1942, and this binder is May." He pulled out a second binder. "June." Then July and August. Each time he put one on the table, dust rose in the air. "I guess I don't have to tell you to be careful, do I?"

"No, sir."

"Good. I'll put them back when you're done."

"Thank you."

He smiled and studied her a moment. "What are you looking for specifically?"

Not knowing him or how long he'd lived in Manchester, Vivien hesitated to tell him. "How long have you been here?" she asked.

"Since 1948. Took over the paper in February."

"You didn't live here in 1942?"

"No." He leaned against the shelf the binders came from. "What happened in '42?"

She explained about finding the scrapbook with articles about a young Japanese girl being found dead in the river. She told him she and her family lived on the farm where the girl and her father worked and lived much of the time.

"Carl McCarthy. He was a widower. Since we live on his old farm now, and after reading all those articles, I wanted to see if anything else happened."

He looked down and seemed to be thinking. Since he didn't live in Manchester when the girl died, Vivien hoped her interest in the girl's death wouldn't bother him. She might need his help to find out more.

"When I first came here," he said, "Mr. Russell, the former editor, told me a bit about the history of Manchester. Mostly about the war years, to be honest. He mentioned the dead girl. He believed Mr. McCarthy innocent, but he didn't dare say anything. Or print anything. Feelings ran pretty high."

"Because the girl was Japanese?"

"Because she was so young."

"The jury convicted McCarthy. I wondered what happened to him?"

"Russell never said. Doesn't your family know anything?"

"Mama left here about then. She and Daddy were courting. He was posted at Camp Forrest. The Army transferred him to Camp Carson soon after they got married. I don't think she heard much about it. My grandma . . . Well, I'm not sure she wants to talk about it." She avoided asking her grandmother, or anyone else who lived there at the time, unless she needed to.

"I'm sure it was traumatic." He turned toward the door. "I'll leave the door open for more light. Hope you find what you want."

"Thanks."

She sat in the chair facing the door and watched him go back down the hall. For a moment, Vivien hoped he might be interested enough to help her find what she needed to know. Oh, well. Time to get busy. She didn't want to rush, but she also didn't want to leave Mama waiting too long at the soda shop. She took the pad and a pencil out of the old purse Mama gave her to use.

The *Manchester Times* paper had few pages, many of those consisting of grocery store ads, obituaries, and sports news. When schools opened, school sports articles made up much of the paper. She scanned the few serious news articles quickly and flipped past those pages.

Mr. Narita found Yoshi's body in May, toward the end of the school year. Mr. McCarthy sent her to New Union Elementary School, the same school Vivien and Lauren attended. The old, cinder block building formed a "U". Classrooms opened onto a raised walkway along the inside of the "U". The walkway stood too high for most students to jump to the ground. Water came from a well. The gym occupied the base of the "U", along with the cafeteria. The best thing about the school was the food they got for lunch. Home cooked meals with locally raised vegetables and meat, prepared and served by women, many with children in the school.

Yoshi had been in the sixth grade, same grade Vivien finished last spring. Mrs. Jenkins might have been her teacher. The first article and many of the following ones recounted the finding of her body floating in the water of the ford. Her father went looking for her earlier in the day. He was quoted as saying he worked in the field across from the house until noon and didn't see her go out. Not one word about when or why she left. Who reported finding her body? Mr. Narita, her father. Mr. McCarthy searched another area.

She wore a dress, not a bathing suit. They assumed a person took her to the river. She swam in the ford before, but not on that day. One article, published before the arrest of Mr. McCarthy, included several interviews with children she went to school with. Some of them weren't shy about expressing animosity toward Yoshi.

"That Nip girl shouldn't have been here. My daddy said so." "No one liked her. She was Japanese." "I'm sorry she's dead, but I'm glad I don't have to go to school with her anymore." Other students described her as shy and smart.

The teachers also described Yoshi as bright and quiet with a good command of English, which other students could learn from. "She spoke little, but she wrote English correctly," her sixth-grade teacher said. The teacher was not named.

Vivien stopped for a moment, considering what the teacher said. The ghost never said a word when she appeared. Why? If she spoke English so well, she shouldn't be shy about explaining what happened. Instead, Vivien must do all this research to find out.

She made notes on the pad and moved on. Maybe Yoshi didn't think Vivien would believe her. Meaning Mr. McCarthy hadn't killed her. Didn't it?

She got through May and started through June when Mr. Logan came back to check on her. "How's it going?"

"All right. I've learned new things." She asked the time. She'd been there forty-five minutes and would have to leave soon.

Mr. Logan disappeared down the hall again. Vivien moved

to July when the trial began and ended. It took only a few days to convict Mr. McCarthy. Many of the townspeople attended the trial, most calling for the accused's blood. He'd said little the whole time, except to protest his innocence. The day before the jury rendered their verdict, he took the stand in his own defense. The reporter quoted it in detail.

"Mr. McCarthy, you decided to send Yoshi Narita to New Union School," his attorney said after establishing Mr. Narita and his daughter lived on the farm. "Why did you go to so much trouble for her?"

"She was a bright girl. She said she missed school. I talked with the principal and we worked it out."

"You liked her?"

"Yes."

"And her father?"

"He was a hard worker. No lollygagging. Spoke only when necessary."

"He was grateful to you? For giving him work and sending his daughter to school?"

"Yes."

Vivien couldn't stay any longer, and she scanned quickly through the balance of Mr. McCarthy's testimony. He denied ever touching the girl. He rarely saw her since she spent time in school and studying in the room she and her father shared.

"No, I didn't kill her," he said when the prosecutor asked.

The lawyer pressed, asking question after question, hardly giving the farmer time to answer. The reporter didn't embellish on the scene, except to show a bit of sympathy for Mr. McCarthy. Or maybe she read it wrong.

She closed the binder and gathered up her things. She stopped in Mr. Logan's office to tell him she'd finished.

"Find what you wanted?"

"I guess. I have to meet Mama, so I didn't read through it

all."

"You raised my own curiosity, so I made a couple of phone calls. I'm sure the information is in later articles, but I thought you'd want to know. They found Mr. McCarthy guilty. I guess you knew."

Vivien nodded.

"After the trial, the judge sentenced him to twenty years in Tennessee State Prison. He may be released next year since he's been on his good behavior."

"Oh. I wondered."

"You may want to be careful about who you talk to in town. I spoke to Mr. Gregory, the attorney who prosecuted him. People don't want McCarthy coming back to Manchester."

She nodded. "Thanks."

She stepped outside. The bright sunlight made her eyes water and she blinked. She hurried toward the other side of the square, hoping to reach the soda shop before Mama. She kept repeating what Mr. Logan said. How many people knew Mr. McCarthy would be getting out of prison early? What would they do if he came back to Manchester?

By the time they released him next year, she and her family would be in France. Would it be far enough to escape the anger of people in town if she kept digging? Would it be soon enough? Grandma would be living here. Mrs. Trent and others already showed how they felt about her asking questions, and they blamed Grandma.

She had to stop. She couldn't let Grandma be hounded because of what she did. Yet, there must be a reason Yoshi appeared to her. Something the dead girl wanted resolved. Either she wanted the farmer to confess or not be released, or if he didn't kill her, she wanted people to know it. If Yoshi and Mr. McCarthy got along like he said in court, it must be she wanted him exonerated.

CHAPTER
FIFTEEN

The phone hung on the wall of the living room. Vivien turned the crank vigorously like she'd seen Grandma do. It made a whirring noise. She stopped and waited until the operator came on the line.

"What number are you calling?"

She stood on tiptoe to reach the mouthpiece. "Please connect me to Mrs. Irma Jenkins."

"Hold please."

While she waited to speak to her teacher, Vivien wondered how much trouble this might cause. She'd asked Grandma how to use the phone. The only other one she'd ever used had a rotary dial with numbers and that was only one time. Mama let her dial the number for her at her aunt's house when they visited two years ago. She felt an excitement at being able to use such wonderful technology.

"Hello." Vivien never spoke to her teacher over the phone and didn't recognize the voice as Mrs. Jenkins'. "Hello. May I speak to Mrs. Jenkins. Please."

"Speaking."

"Hello. This is Vivien Brewer."

"Vivien? Why on earth are you callin'?"

She explained about living in Mr. McCarthy's place and finding the scrapbook. Before she called, she tried to think of a good reason for her interest, one which would appeal to her teacher. She told her living in the same house made her wonder what happened to Yoshi Narita.

"Those newspaper articles should tell you all you need to know." Her voice became a little less friendly.

"I know. But they don't tell me what she was like. Did the other students like her? Was she smart? Did she —"

"You should dwell on more important things."

"Can you at least tell me if she had any friends?"

"She had no friends. She was Japanese. No one liked her."

"Mr. McCarthy did."

"And you saw what happened to her because of him."

"You believe he killed her."

"Of course. He was convicted."

"Do you know if she went to the ford to swim?"

"I do not. I have nothing further to say."

"Thank you, Mrs. Jenkins." The line went dead.

Vivien hung up the receiver and stood thinking. Disappointment brought tears to her eyes. She considered Mrs. Jenkins a wonderful teacher and felt certain she would be more willing to tell her what Yoshi was like.

If a nice woman like Mrs. Jenkins got upset at her asking questions, she could only expect the same from others. How could she find out what happened and what Yoshi wanted if no one would talk to her?

Frustrated, she stomped out the front door and sat on the swing trying to think. Who else could she talk to? So far, Mrs. O'Shea was helpful in finding information. Mr. Logan was willing to discuss what happened but he didn't live there at the time.

The screen door opened, and Mama called out, "Come on, girls. We're going to the hospital now." Grandma's friend, Mrs. Fletcher, needed an operation.

Vivien went inside where they all gathered in the living room. "We're going in the Chevy," Mama said.

"Don't you think the girls should put on some clothes," Grandma said. "They're half naked."

"They're all right, Mama. Young girls wear shorts when they go into town these days."

Mama had told Grandma that more than once since they came to live with her. In the heat, Vivien couldn't imagine wearing more clothes, except on Sundays. Grandma wore stockings held up with garters she rolled up to the top of each stocking. Her dress reached half-way down her calf. A small hat sat on top of her head. She harumphed and picked up her purse from the kitchen table.

Vivien sat quietly in the back seat, trying to come up with an idea for finding more information about Yoshi without causing trouble. Nothing came to mind by the time they reached the single-story hospital and went inside. Since she was twelve years old, they allowed Vivien to go to the room with Mama and Grandma, but Lauren had to sit in the waiting room. She'd brought her current book, so she didn't much care.

Vivien met Mrs. Fletcher right after they moved to Manchester. She reminded her of Mrs. Warner in Breckinridge and liked her immediately. Grandma hugged the patient lying in the bed, looking pale against the white sheets. Otherwise, she didn't look terribly ill. Grandma said she needed a serious operation but not exactly what it was.

"When is the operation, Ellen?" Grandma asked.

"First thing tomorrow."

"Is your daughter able to come?"

"No, she's working, and they won't let her take time off."

Grandma said she'd come and be with her.

"You know what I'd like right now? A Coca Cola. They don't have any here and won't get me one from the service station down the street."

"I'll do it," Vivien said.

"No, it's a little too far to walk in this heat," Grandma said. "Your mother and I will go in the car." She and her friend exchanged a look as if they shared a secret.

She liked Mrs. Fletcher, but Vivien didn't feel comfortable staying alone with her at first. The first few minutes they said nothing. Mrs. Fletcher lay back, eyes closed.

"What have you been up to this summer?" she asked suddenly.

"Not much. Swimming. Reading."

"I heard you've been causing a bit of a stir in town."

"What?"

"Come sit down on the bed." Vivien did. "You're looking around about the Yoshi Narita girl."

Vivien looked down at her hands in her lap, expecting another scolding. Mrs. Fletcher patted her hands, and Vivien looked up. "I taught at New Union Elementary for twenty years. I retired in 1946. I knew Yoshi. It broke my heart when they found her."

"Do you believe Mr. McCarthy killed her?"

"No. Carl was a kind, lonely man who adored the girl. She adored him."

"Did her father resent him?"

"Ah, you're wondering if he was jealous. No. Well, it was hard to tell what he might be thinking or feeling. He never showed any emotion or reaction, the times I saw him. Someone did resent her."

"Who?" Vivien almost whispered the question.

"Her name is Shelby Adair. Her father is a big man in the county. Wealthy. Gets what he wants to this day. Shelby always got whatever she wanted, too."

"Was she jealous of Yoshi?" The name Adair sounded familiar.

"Yes. Oh, not of her looks — both were pretty girls, one blonde, the other with coal black hair — but of her intelligence. Until Yoshi came, Shelby considered herself the smartest kid in school. A teacher or two told her that and Mrs. Jenkins doted on her."

Mrs. Fletcher shifted on the bed and grimaced in pain. She lay back on the pillows, catching her breath. Another moment and she leaned toward Vivien.

"I need to tell you before they come back. Shelby made Yoshi's life miserable in school. She taunted her for being Japanese and being short. Shelby, tall for her age, towered over Yoshi. She led other girls in taunting and . . ." She sighed. "And being rough with her. One time I saw them shove her down during recess.

"After they found her body, I overheard Shelby telling the other girls, those who followed her around, they better not tell anyone what happened. She didn't say what happened, but so soon after . . ."

She winced again.

"You didn't tell anyone then?"

The woman shook her head. "Her father could have destroyed me. I was a widow with two children. I couldn't chance losing my job. But I want someone to know now, in case." She sighed. "I've always been ashamed I didn't speak up then."

"Does Shelby live here now?"

"Yeah, her and a couple of her followers. Shelby married

Buddy Dulaney. He works for her daddy. He's a bully and people in town are afraid of him. It's no secret he sees a lot of other women. Maybe Shelby's punishment for whatever she did."

Mama's voice came from down the hall. Vivien and Mrs. Fletcher exchanged a glance.

"Thanks," Vivien said.

Mama's voice grew closer. Mrs. Fletcher took Vivien's hand. "Something died inside Carl when Yoshi died. When they arrested him and put him on trial, he didn't care at all."

Mama and Grandma appeared in the doorway, each holding a bottle of Coca Cola. Mama held one to Mrs. Fletcher. A nurse passed by the door. She stepped inside.

"Mrs. Fletcher, you know you can't have a Coke so close to your surgery."

"Just this one."

"No, ma'am."

Before the nurse could take the bottles away, Mama held them out to Vivien. "Go drink these with Lauren."

CHAPTER
SIXTEEN

Next afternoon, Mama brought Grandma home from the hospital. Their eyes were red and they sniffed back tears. "Mrs. Fletcher died on the operating table," Mama said.

"Why?" Lauren asked.

"The cancer spread too far, honey," Mama said. "They couldn't save her."

"Oh." No one said the word cancer before.

Grandma went to her room to lie down. Mama changed clothes and puttered around the house. Lauren tried to ask more questions. "Not now," Mama said.

Vivien went out on the back porch where she usually went when she needed to think or wanted to be alone. Everything — the well and smokehouse, the barn in the distance, the woods behind — it all seemed so old, almost magical. And quiet.

She couldn't comprehend Mrs. Fletcher's dying. She talked to her yesterday. She liked her. And she wanted to talk to her again about Yoshi. It would never happen. Sadness settled over her, and she believed she would miss Mrs. Fletcher, in spite of only seeing her a few times.

Last night, thinking over what she said, Vivien felt angry with Mrs. Fletcher for not helping Yoshi. A girl her own age, with no friends, in a strange country. Someone should have helped her. Mr. McCarthy might have if he knew. He let them live in his house instead of in camp. It occurred to her, if Yoshi and her father stayed at the camp, she might not have died.

She sat watching the trees move with the breeze. She saw Yoshi sitting in the same place. A schoolbook in her lap. Both her father and Mr. McCarthy working in the field across the road, hoeing between rows of corn.

Shelby and three other girls from school came around the corner of the house, laughing and talking. "There you are," Shelby said. "We came to take you swimming with us down at the ford."

"Thank you, no," Yoshi said. "I must ask my father."

"Go ask him," another girl said. The four of them giggled.

"He is in field with Mr. McCarthy."

"Okay. Come with us anyway. They'll never know."

"No, I —"

"Sure, you can. We just want to cool off."

Yoshi opened her mouth to protest. Instead of her voice, Vivien heard Lauren coming out of the house calling Vivien's name. The scene faded.

"What do you want?" Anger made her words sharp.

"Mama says we can go to the ford if we want."

"I don't want."

"Come on, Viv. I can't go by myself."

Vivien shook her head. "I don't feel like it today," she said more gently.

"You're sad about Mrs. Fletcher being dead?"

"Yeah. She was a nice lady."

"I remember meeting her one time before." Lauren jumped off the porch and whirled around. "Does everyone die?"

"I guess so."

"I don't want to die. I don't want any of us to die."

"Me neither."

Lauren went off around the corner of the house, probably to the swing. Vivien figured the mailman should have passed. She walked around to the mailbox standing beside the driveway and pulled the metal door down. She found several letters — including one from Daddy — and a Sears and Roebuck catalog. She loved going through the catalog for hours, making a list of what she wanted. Clothes, shoes, purses, pretty things for a bedroom she didn't have. They couldn't afford any of it, but they didn't call it a "wish book" for nothing.

The letter from Daddy would cheer everyone up and she raced into the house to tell Mama. She found her asleep in the bedroom. Grandma, too. No way would she open the letter herself no matter how much she wanted to. She put the stack of mail on the kitchen table and sat down to look through the catalog. She got back up to fetch her tablet and a pencil and poured herself a glass of sweet tea. Mama found her there, an hour later, one page of the tablet nearly filled with page numbers, item name, item number and price.

Mama's face brightened when Vivien handed her the letter from Daddy. She took it into the bedroom to read by herself. Later, she would read it to the girls. But she wanted the private things to herself.

When Grandma got up, she and Mama made an early dinner. They'd missed lunch and the girls were famished. They set the table. Fried cabbage stunk up the house and made their mouths water. They also ate fried potatoes and corn bread. More sweet iced tea quenched their thirst.

Once they finished washing the dishes and cleaned up the kitchen, they all sat at the table for Mama to read Daddy's letter. They drank more tea and listened raptly.

It finally warmed up a couple weeks ago. It's cooler here than in Tennessee. Everything's green now and poppies are blooming.

I'll be going to Germany next week for TDY (temporary duty) and should be back in Fontenet two weeks after that. The new lieutenant seems like a good guy, but don't know [Mama cleared her throat] *nothing about being a soldier.*

I think I've found a house to rent. Two bedrooms, large kitchen, and a yard. It is not too far from post.

The Communists demonstrated in a small village between Fontenet and La Rochelle. The main PX is in La Rochelle, and we'll do shopping there. The Army tells us not to stop in that village.

He sent his love and kisses for Mama and the girls, and a thank you for Mama's letter. Vivien went out on the back porch to read. *Only two bedrooms.* She and Lauren would be sharing a room again.

She'd gotten another book on French history from the library and she searched for any mention of Fontenet. She found nothing at all and checked the copyright date. 1940. Maybe she needed a newer book.

The library must have a gazetteer or an atlas so she could find those towns on the map of France. From what Daddy said, though, Fontenet was small, and she guessed it might not be on a map. She wished she'd paid more attention to geography lessons.

Vivien went inside and found Mama mending a torn hem in one of Lauren's blouses.

"Mama."

"Yes?" She looked up from her sewing.

"How will we get to France?"

"Daddy hasn't said. By boat or plane."

"A ship? A big one, like the Titanic?"

"Well, hopefully a ship that won't sink, but yes."

"Or a plane. Flying."

Mama smiled. "Yes. Exciting, isn't it?"

Vivien sat down in another chair. Yes, exciting. She'd been on a train once. But they always drove when they moved from one place to another. Come October, they'd either be flying over the Atlantic Ocean or sailing on it. Which did she want most?

CHAPTER
SEVENTEEN

At the library on Saturday, Vivien gathered together the last two books on France. She'd read all the rest, especially the pictures. She pulled out books with maps from the reference section, intending to look for places in France Daddy mentioned in his letter. Mama wrote down the names, so she knew how to spell them. Reference books must be read in the library, but she had to do something else first.

She tentatively approached the desk. Mrs. O'Shea gave her a dark look when she came into the building. It took a few moments for Vivien to gather up courage enough to approach her.

"Good afternoon, Mrs. O'Shea."

"How can I help you?" Her voice sounded more friendly than the look earlier, and Vivien wondered if she'd been mistaken.

"Do you know where Shelby Dulaney lives? Mrs. Jenkins suggested I talk with her."

"About what?"

"About when she had Mrs. Jenkins for her teacher in the

sixth grade. You know, what it was like back then. Mrs. Jenkins said we would have to write an essay on Tennessee history in the seventh grade, and I thought I would do one on the school."

The librarian looked interested. "I believe she lives just off the McMinnville Highway. The big white house with black shutters. She has horses in the field."

"I know it. Or I've seen it. Thank you."

Mrs. O'Shea nodded. Vivian walked back to the table where she and Lauren always sat. The old purse and her writing pad and pencils sat waiting for her.

She sat in the chair opposite Lauren who didn't even notice her return. She was engrossed in *War of the Worlds* by H.G. Wells. After Vivien introduced her little sister to science fiction books, she became so fond of the genre she read little else. Luckily for them, the library shelved all of the science fiction in the children's fiction stacks.

It was one of Vivien's favorite kind of stories, too, having read all of Wells' and Verne's novels. She'd found other authors, but she also liked historical fiction, books on history, and the occasional romance. She'd read several of Mama's collection from the Book of the Month Club, which didn't seem to have a genre of their own.

With her current interest in France, she scrounged through the card catalog for books, fiction and non-fiction about the country. She'd discovered Eleanor of Aquitaine, mother of Richard the Lion Hearted, who reigned as queen in both France and England.

She located Aquitaine on the map of France in the atlas before looking for Fontenet. She took Mama's note out of the purse with the town names and opened it up. It didn't appear in the list of towns and cities on the maps, but she found La Rochelle, a large city on the Atlantic coast, not far from Fontenet according to Daddy. Would they land there if they went by ship? Where would they land if they flew by plane?

The now familiar shape appeared off to her right and she turned. Yoshi stood a few feet away, holding out her hand, pleading.

No, I haven't forgotten you. I have other things I need to do.

The girl turned and walked away, her form fading until she disappeared. Vivian felt guilty. Maybe she should check out France and where they would live later. Or maybe finding out about Yoshi's death could wait. After all, she'd been dead fifteen years.

Vivien turned back to the books. She could at least see if she could find their new home on the map. The only reference Daddy gave for the location of Fontenet was its nearness to La Rochelle. She turned to another Gazetteer and found the map of France. She placed her index finger on La Rochelle and slowly circled outward from there. According to the scale, she'd searched over 150 miles but couldn't find the name. Could it be so small? Why would the Army have a post in such a small place?

The names looked strange and difficult to pronounce. How did the French people pronounce them? If she learned to speak French . . . Did they say things so differently? She knew the word. "oui," meant "yes," having figured it out from the Mouse Musketeers in a Tom & Jerry comic book, but nothing else.

She set the gazetteer aside and opened the larger atlas. The map of France spanned two pages and seemed detailed enough to show smaller towns. But no Fontenet. The best she could say, it lay in the western part of the country and not too far from the Atlantic Ocean.

Time to give up on the maps. Maybe she could find books on the language. A French dictionary. Or maybe a French textbook. If schools use English textbooks, there must be books for teaching French.

Yoshi appeared beside the table, again. She shoved the large books off the table. They landed with a bang and slid across the floor. Lauren yelped. Vivien jumped up and looked from the books to Yoshi who faded and disappeared.

Mrs. O'Shea rushed up. "What on earth is happening?" She looked scary mad.

"Sorry, Mrs. O'Shea. It was an accident." Vivien bent down to pick them up. "They slipped out of my hands."

The librarian crossed her arms over her chest. "You two need to be more careful."

"I didn't do anything," Lauren said.

The librarian stalked off. Why was she so angry? Neither Vivien nor Lauren did anything, but she couldn't know about the ghost. Vivien remembered she wanted to look for a book on the French language. She didn't find anything in the card catalog, so she went to the desk to ask for help.

"French?" Mrs. O'Shea said. "No, we don't have any books on foreign languages. You'd probably need to go to Nashville for something like that."

Vivien thanked her and started back toward the table. She turned around instead. "Mrs. O'Shea, are you angry at me?"

"What? No. About those books? It startled me is all."

"Good. I don't want to make you mad."

The librarian shook her head and smiled. "I have some things on my mind, is all. I'm not . . ." She shook her head again. "Manchester is a small town. Little things get blown out of proportion."

"Yes, ma'am." Vivien thanked her and went back to the table. She felt like Mrs. O'Shea had been about to say something important. *Did she stop because I'm a kid?*

The time came for Mama and Grandma to pick them up.

The two of them carried their stacks of books to the front desk. The car sat near the entrance when they walked outside. The sun beat down on them as they walked over.

"Vivien almost got us kicked out of the library," Lauren said after they got in the back seat.

"What?" Mama said. "What did you do?" She turned around to look at Vivien.

"Nothing. A couple of books slipped out of my hands and fell on the floor. They made an awful noise, and Mrs. O'Shea got mad."

"You shouldn't be so careless," Mama said. She put the car in gear and drove out of the parking lot. "She let you check out books anyway, I see."

"Yes, ma'am. I wanted to look for books on French, but she said they don't have any."

"It's a small library," Mama said.

"Can we find a bigger library? She said the Nashville library might have some."

"Not nearby. That's a long way to go. I doubt anyone in Manchester would be interested."

"Why should they?" Grandma said. "People should learn to speak English." She called people in cars with out-of-state license plates, "foreigners."

"But, Mama, we'll be living in their country."

"Don't matter," Grandma said.

Vivien sat back, thinking hard about what Grandma said. What did she think about people in this country speaking Japanese? She suspected Japanese sounded more foreign even than French ever would. But Yoshi did speak English. She spoke a little funny but . . .

She never spoke when she appeared. But the teachers said she spoke as good as some Americans. As well as, she corrected herself. Did a lot of people in Manchester feel the same way? They should speak English?

When they first moved back to Manchester, a few people, even Grandma, remarked on how they talked. Mama had mostly lost her southern accent. Daddy, born in "Yankee land," never spoke with an accent. The kids in school teased Vivien and Lauren the first few days, but either they spoke more like them after a time, or the other kids got used to hearing them.

Mr. Narita wasn't much of a talker, people said. If the way he and his daughter spoke bothered the locals, how much would other differences make them more unwelcome?

She stared out the window, watching the scenery flash by. Not far from town, they passed Shelby Dulaney's big house. Vivien's vision turned inward, and she saw Yoshi on the back porch of Grandma's house again, the other girls trying to talk her into going to the ford. Vivien felt the girl's resolve weaken. She wanted to go, but Father would not like it if she did not get his permission.

Vivien studied the girls. The clear leader stood slightly taller than the others. Her blond ponytail shone in the afternoon sun. The girl standing beside her looked rounder, heavier, with short brown hair. The two behind them looked pretty, their long brown hair in ponytails of different lengths. They smiled to encourage Yoshi to go with them.

The blonde turned her head slightly and looked straight at Vivien. *Stay out of this. It's none of your business.*

Vivien jerked. Her heart beat faster. Mama turned off the highway onto the dirt road. The hot sun shining through the window did not warm her.

CHAPTER
EIGHTEEN

Vivien propped the bicycle against the raised porch. She'd borrowed it from Emily at the store who used it to make deliveries.

She hadn't ridden a bike in years, since before they moved to Kentucky. They'd gotten rid of a lot of stuff so moving wouldn't cost so much. At first, she had trouble coordinating her movements, but it came back to her. Muscles remembered how to balance. They also protested by the time she arrived at her destination.

The doorbell echoed in a large space behind the door when she pressed the button. She stood back, taking in the front of the large house. Similar, two-story houses could be found all over the South. Mama called them Colonial. This one didn't look as large and grand as most others.

Black shutters on either side of the windows and the door broke up the whiteness. The smell of newly cut grass wafted up from the lawn. A few bushes stood against the porch, which ran the width of the house. A couple of rocking chairs sat to the right, looking as if they'd never been used. It made Grandma's place look derelict. The trailer even more so.

The door opened and a black woman said, "May I help you?"

"Y-yes, ma'am. My name's Vivien Brewer. I-I wondered if Mrs. Dulaney might be home." She tried to call to make an appointment, but no one ever answered.

"Come in, chil'. I'll see if Miz Dulaney is available."

She stepped into the coolness of a large foyer and onto a dark blue rug. This, her first experience with a black servant, made her uncomfortable. She'd seen movies and heard talk about such, but never encountered the situation in person. How did one act? She tried to remember the movies, but nothing came to her.

The woman disappeared through an open doorway at the far end. Closed doors on the right side of the space must open into different rooms. A staircase rose to the second floor against the wall on the left. Paintings hung on the walls, one landscape over a bench against the wall to her right. She considered sitting on the bench but decided not to. It might not be proper.

Footsteps approached from the back and soon a woman appeared. She drew nearer and Vivien froze. The girl, taller than her friends, with blond hair. All grown up, she looked almost the same, only a little curvier. Even the smile on her lips, but not in her eyes.

"How may I help you?" she asked in a full southern drawl. "Some sort of fund raising?"

"No, ma'am. My . . . my name is Vivien Brewer. I go to New Union Elementary School. My teacher, Mrs. Jenkins, thought you might help me."

"Heavens to Betsy. Is she still there?"

"Yes, ma'am."

"Come on in. We're puttin' up blackberry jam." She led the way through the dining room at the back and into the kitchen. "You like blackberry jam?"

"Yes, ma'am." The smell of blackberries filled the room, bringing memories of Mama doing the same at Camp Breckinridge.

Vivien worried about how to raise the questions she wanted to ask. She'd given it a lot of thought the past few days. An idea came to her while riding the bicycle this morning.

Fans blew from several angles in the kitchen, where pots boiled on the large stove. Vivien never saw anything like it. When Mama made blackberry jam in Breckinridge, the smaller stove in the trailer with four burners had been big enough. Here, two more black servants worked on cooking, sterilizing, filling, and sealing.

"Can y'all do without me for a bit?" Mrs. Dulaney asked.

The black ladies smiled and nodded. Vivien suspected they did all the work, and Mrs. Dulaney "supervised."

She motioned for Vivien to follow her through the kitchen and into a small, intimate room to the left. Outside the window looking out onto the back yard stood an ancient weeping willow. Its shade fell on the corner of the house. "This is where I come to relax," she said. "It's cooler and quieter." She fell onto a velvet sofa and indicated an overstuffed chair. "Have a seat."

The chair looked like it could swallow her up and Vivien sat tentatively. Within seconds, she sat back. The comfort of the chair wrapped around her. She didn't sink in as she'd feared. The softness of the seat held her up. Definitely a chair to relax in. If only she could take it home to sit in while she read.

"Now, what can I do for you?" The woman smiled, as vacantly as before.

"Like I said, Mrs. Jenkins thought you might be able to help me with an essay on Tennessee history I'm hoping to write when I'm in the seventh grade. She said it's a standard assignment each year and I wanted to get ahead. My family will be leaving Manchester this fall, but I'd like to earn extra credit before changing schools."

"My goodness. Where will you be moving to?"

"Daddy is in the Army and we're going to France."

"How exciting." For the first time, she seemed interested. "How long will y'all be there?"

"He's already there. Mama and us girls will be there two years."

Mrs. Dulaney seemed to be thinking of something else and for a moment Vivien wondered if she'd forgotten about her.

"Anyway," she said abruptly.

"I've been reading and found out about the prisoners held at Camp Forrest," Vivien continued. "We live in Mr. McCarthy's old house. My grandpa bought the farm during the war." Mrs. Dulaney's expression changed. Her eyes cut sharply to stare at Vivien. "He had a Japanese man and his daughter staying with him for a while. I wondered if you could tell me anything about them."

"Why would you think I'd know anything?"

"You went to school with her. Her name was Yoshi."

"I know her name."

The change in the woman frightened Vivien. She'd looked pretty before. Now, her face screwed up in anger. Maybe hatred. She looked like she would jump off the sofa at any minute, yet she stayed seated. Vivien recoiled, ready to jump up and run out.

Silence lengthened between them until the woman finally looked away. Vivien moved the purse from beside her onto her lap. She took out the pencil and the pad of paper, needing distraction.

"I – I only wondered what it was like," Vivien said. "Having prisoners in the area. Going to the schools."

"We all made sacrifices for the war." Mrs. Dulaney stared out the window.

Vivien groaned inwardly. She should have come around to the subject of Yoshi more subtly.

"The school hasn't changed much," the woman said softly. "The buildin', the kids, too, I s'pose."

"Did y'all have what you needed for class?"

"No. So much went to the war effort. We saved our pennies so we could buy savings stamps. We put them in a book and once we filled it, we could get a war bond." A smile touched her lips. "So many soldiers came into town from Camp Forrest, looking handsome in their uniforms. Most mamas protected their daughters, especially ones as young as me. Some got into . . ." She looked at Vivien. "Those who were old enough, went out with the soldiers. To the movies or out for a soda. They had money and could buy things the rest of us had trouble finding. Sugar. Cigarettes."

Now she'd begun reminiscing, Mrs. Dulaney relaxed and talked freely. Vivien asked questions to steer the conversation more to the school. What the woman felt about the school at the time, she couldn't tell. She seemed to remember it fondly.

"Did you and your friends go to the ford to swim on hot days?"

"Yes, a bunch of us . . . Why are you askin' about the ford?"

"My sister and I go swimming there. Sometimes, we take a bar of soap and wash up." Embarrassment followed her statement, as if she'd admitted her family couldn't afford modern plumbing.

"Oh, we never bathed in the ford. But a few of us did go swimmin' there. The public pool was closed because of the polio scare and people didn't have swimmin' pools in their back yards like they do today. My daddy gave me an old Ford he let me drive on back roads and a bunch of us would pile in and go to the ford."

So, in the vision, they got to the farm in an old car. Vivien had wondered. Walking that distance on a hot summer day would have been too much for almost anyone.

"It was jus' us girls. No boys allowed. We loved the privacy, bein' on our own."

A cloud passed over her face.

"Did Yoshi ever go with you?"

Again, the sharp, angry look. "Do you think we wanted a Nip girl to come with us? Bad enough they made us go to school with her. Those Nips acted worse than the Germans in the camp."

"They caused trouble?"

"They did. Kept claimin' they were Americans. They came here from California. People are strange enough there, anyway."

"But Yoshi never went swimming with y'all?" Vivien asked.

"Oh, maybe once or twice. We didn't make a habit of it."

"She must have been lonely."

"She and her father should have stayed in the camp," Mrs. Dulaney said. "Not come wandering around here."

"People must have been sad when they found her dead in the river."

"Most of us were glad she wasn't around anymore. Her and that creepy father of hers. Never spoke to anyone, hardly."

"People blamed Mr. McCarthy."

"He brought the two of 'em here. He got what he deserved, too."

"Did you know Yoshi went to the ford alone?"

"I thought you wanted to know about the school. Why all these questions about the Nip girl?"

Vivien felt herself blush. "Sorry. It sounded interesting."

She asked a few more questions about going to school at New Union during the war. While Mrs. Dulaney gave a long rambling answer to one of the questions, Vivien saw familiar movement outside one of the windows. She looked over to see Yoshi's pale face pressed against the glass, her gaze glued to Mrs. Dulaney. How often did the ghost peer into the house, watching the woman who may have been the girl's murderer? Did Mrs. Dulaney ever sense her presence?

"Excuse me, Miz Dulaney," a voice said from the door.

"Yes, Hildy?"

"We done used up all the jars, and there's a pile more of jam."

"I'll be right there." Mrs. Dulaney stood and looked down at Vivien. "Good luck with your essay." She walked toward the doorway but turned back. "Don't come here again."

Vivien stood and followed. Everything about the woman felt cold, as if she faked her southern hospitality. The warning not to return sent chills through her, even the heat in the kitchen couldn't warm.

"Hildy, would you please show our guest to the door."

"Thank you," Vivien said and followed Hildy from the kitchen. The servant opened the front door and stood aside. "Thanks, Hildy."

Vivien stepped out into the sun's rays. She couldn't see for several seconds and stood blinking her eyes until they adjusted to the glare. Next time they went into town, she needed to buy herself a pair of sunglasses.

The air got hotter while she sat with Mrs. Dulaney. It touched the skin, but not the chill inside.

Cycling back made her sweat more than ever. At the store, she shared a Nehi orange soda with Emily. She thanked her friend for the use of the bicycle and walked the rest of the way home. With each step, she became more convinced she'd done the wrong thing, visiting the one person who seemed to have hated Yoshi most.

If Mrs. Dulaney had anything to do with the girl's death, what would she do to prevent anyone finding out?

CHAPTER
NINETEEN

The sun went down and the world dimmed. The dark outline of the trees against the sky swayed in a breeze which didn't reach the porch. The heat bore down, but it was so much worse inside of the house. The four of them would wait for the bedrooms to cool down. The difference would be only slight.

"Listen," Mama said. "An owl."

Whooo. Whooo.

Vivien perked up. She'd never heard an owl before. She waited for it to hoot again, but only heard the buzzing of mosquitoes and tree frogs. They each held a last glass of sweet tea for the day. It felt cool going down and drops of condensation falling onto her bare thigh made Vivien wish she could pour the glass over her head.

Fireflies twinkled all over the yard, but no one had the energy to chase them. Vivien's mind re-ran her visit with Mrs. Dulaney. She'd accomplished nothing except to make the woman angry, maybe suspicious. No way could she try to talk to her again. What if she called Mrs. Jenkins to see if the teacher actually suggested Vivien talk with her?

The young woman acted strange. Distracted maybe. More than that, she seemed unhappy. Maybe she did know about her husband running around. Or did she wish she had children, which might keep her husband home? Maybe she regretted what happened to Yoshi, but it didn't seem likely. Her response on hearing the girl's name sounded brutal.

Vivien told Mama about the conversation and described how Mrs. Dulaney acted. "You may be right," Mama said. "She sounds unhappy."

"You'd best stay away from that woman," Grandma said. "Her daddy is a powerful man. He won't tolerate anyone messin' with her."

"Then why doesn't he do something about that husband of hers?" Mama asked. "He goes out at night. Tullahoma. Nashville. Drinking and carousing."

"We don't interfere in affairs between a man and his wife," Grandma said. "Ellen told me he thinks Shelby doesn't behave like a wife should, so her husband will stay home." Ellen Kittrell, mother of Emily and Jean. Grandma occasionally ordered a few things from their store, which Emily delivered on her bicycle.

"Doesn't give a man the right . . ." Mama said.

The conversation died. Vivien decided not to think about Shelby Dulaney anymore. Instead, she listened for the owl. Only the singing of tree frogs and various bugs disturbed the silence.

Grandma went in to bed first. The others followed soon after. Mama tucked the girls in. She sat on the edge of the bed.

"Viv, are you sure about what you're doing? I don't want you getting into trouble like you did in Breckinridge."

"It's important, Mama. I don't think Mr. McCarthy killed

the Japanese girl. Mrs. Dulaney hated Yoshi. I don't know why, exactly. But Yoshi wants me to find out. I have to do it."

"Why doesn't she simply tell you?"

Vivien shrugged. "Maybe she doesn't know."

"You know I can't interfere. Same as my mama couldn't interfere when I went through the same things. I grew out of it and you will, too."

"I know."

Mama leaned down and kissed her forehead. "'Night."

After what happened with the ghosts at Camp Breckinridge, and they were all safely moved to Grandma's, Mama explained about talking with ghosts. About how the same thing happened to her and Grandma, too. Maybe it did have to do with having her first menstrual period. Maybe the increase in hormones opened their minds and other perceptions.

Grandma had told Mama about the same thing happening to her at about the same age. Her mother, Vivien's great-grandmother, didn't interfere, either. Interfering harms the girl, she explained. She must handle the situation on her own, except in rare instances of possible violence. Eventually the ability faded and disappeared. Until then, Vivien must face it on her own.

Mama got into her bed and soon snored softly.

"Viv," Lauren said.

"Huh?" Vivien said, startled. She thought her little sister was asleep.

"Do you like seeing ghosts?"

"I don't know. It's kind of exciting. But it scares me, too. Yoshi isn't like Nurse Armstrong. I don't think she would hurt me."

"Who's Yoshi."

Vivien didn't answer and Lauren lay quietly for a time. Vivien considered the question. Did she like seeing ghosts and helping them? Did she wish she didn't have to?

"Viv, do you think it will happen to me when I'm as old as you?"

"I don't think so. They said it happens to only one girl in each generation."

"Why you and not me?"

"I don't know. Can't be because I'm the eldest, since Mama's the youngest, but she could see them."

Why did she have the ability? Mama didn't know. Neither did Grandma. Strange how it worked out.

Lauren stopped asking questions, and Vivien drifted off to sleep. She didn't know what time it was when she sat up in bed, panting for breath. She'd dreamed of being at the ford. Something heavy hit her from behind, and she fell forward into the water. Whatever hit her pressed against her back. She couldn't get up. She needed to get up. She couldn't breathe.

She gasped for air. Her face was dry when she pressed both hands against her cheeks. Her breathing slowed and she got out of bed and used the chamber pot. Barefoot, she went out on the back porch. The felt air warm and soft around her. She listened to the silence. Nothing from tree frogs or mosquitos, only the owl hooted in the trees behind the house. The eerie sound repeated twice. She shivered and went back to bed.

CHAPTER
TWENTY

"Quit moping," Mama said. "Work on your crocheting or read a book."

Vivien groaned softly. Mama taught her the basics of crocheting right after school closed for the summer. She still had a lot to learn. It kept her busy when she didn't have her nose in a book, sat thinking on the back porch, or on the swing in the front yard.

Mama heard on the radio the day before about another polio outbreak. People associated coming down with the disease with swimming in middle to late summer. She told the girls they couldn't go swimming for a while.

"But, Mama, we got the vaccine," Vivien said.

"I don't want to take any chances."

For all of her young life, swimming in summer became equated with catching the dreaded polio. Newspapers printed pictures of children in iron lungs, able to breathe only with the help of the machine. Others couldn't walk without crutches and braces. A man named Salk developed a vaccine to halt the disease. Nearly everyone got the shot and breathed a sigh of relief. Then, people became frightened when vaccinated children came down with it, but in a few months, the number of cases decreased.

An occasional small outbreak would be reported every year, but the reports came out of fear more than actual cases. It happened often enough for mothers to warn their children about swimming. And without swimming, the girls had little else to do.

So, the two of them moped about. They'd read all of the books from the library and they exaggerated suffering from the heat, although the discomfort was real enough.

Vivian considered looking through the scrapbook again, but she'd almost memorized the articles. She went into the bedroom and pulled the cigar box from under the bed, opening it on her lap. Carefully, she took everything out and placed the items in two rows on the quilt. She picked up the lock of hair and clutched it tightly. She closed her eyes.

A strong feeling of love came over her, chased away by a rush of sorrow. She'd always guessed Mr. McCarthy got the lock of hair when he took Yoshi to get her hair cut. Now, she wondered if it might have been cut after she died.

If only she knew someone to talk to, someone who didn't fear remembering or telling what they knew about Yoshi and her death. Only two people talked to her willingly about it. Mrs. Fletcher, now gone. And Mr. Logan, who didn't live in Manchester at the time.

Mrs. O'Shea didn't live in Manchester back then, either, and probably knew nothing about it, except what she'd been told. Vivien wondered if some of those who did live in town then might have warned the librarian against helping Vivien gather information.

Mrs. Jenkins claimed not to know much, even though she taught both Yoshi and Shelby in class. How could she convince the teacher to tell her more? But if someone else killed Yoshi, no one would want to talk about it. Especially if the culprit turned out to be Shelby Dulaney.

Vivien would never be convinced Mr. McCarthy killed the girl. She'd considered the possibility Mr. Narita did it, but it seemed a ridiculous notion. And her ghost led Vivien to believe the girls took her to the ford and drowned her. The four had been led by Shelby. Were the others willing participants?

But who found her? Vivien couldn't remember. She reached for the scrapbook, then remembered. When she went missing, Mr. McCarthy and Mr. Narita searched for her. Mr. McCarthy went to the fields, Mr. Narita to the ford.

Vivien picked up each item and replaced it in the cigar box. She picked up the report card. Mrs. Jenkins could be a tough teacher, but the grades she gave Yoshi reflected honesty. The teacher hadn't liked the girl, at least she gave that impression. However, she earned As and Bs, even in English.

Did Mrs. Jenkins have mixed feelings toward Yoshi? She acted like she didn't like the girl because of her race. Maybe it was more because of Shelby and her family. Mrs. Fletcher never spoke up out of fear of losing her job. Might the same be true of Mrs. Jenkins? Even after so much time had passed.

Saturday came and the girls were back in the library, searching the bookshelves for their next haul. They each placed two piles on their favorite table. One to check out and take home. One to look through in the library until Mama came to pick them up.

Vivien always felt happy among the books. She could live in the building, given the chance. She'd already browsed fiction and made her way to the history section and found the shelves with ancient Egyptian history. She'd become interested in it after reading an article on the Valley of the Kings in *National Geographic*. She turned a corner and spotted Mrs. Jenkins looking over the selection of American history. She hesitated only a moment to take advantage of the luck which brought her teacher here on the same day.

"Hi, Mrs. Jenkins."

The woman jumped and turned to look at who spoke. "Oh, hello, Vivien. You startled me."

"I'm sorry. I didn't mean to."

"You're getting books to read?"

"Yes, ma'am. We come on Saturdays. Could I ask you a question?"

"What about?"

Vivien hesitated again.

"If it's about Yoshi Narita, I've told you all I care to."

"Please, Mrs. Jenkins. My curiosity is killing me."

"I doubt that."

"I only want to know what she was like. Mr. McCarthy left all these newspaper articles and a cigar box with stuff."

"What kind of stuff?" Mrs. Jenkins appeared interested all of a sudden.

"There's a picture of Yoshi. Her report card. A lock of her hair."

"Her hair?"

"Yeah."

Mrs. Jenkins frowned.

"I mean," Vivien said, "yes, ma'am. And a few other things. I don't know what it all means."

"It means Mr. McCarthy was a sick man." She broke eye contact and studied the spines of books on a shelf at eye level.

"You believe he hurt her?"

"Of course."

"But I feel like he loved her so much."

"Too much, you mean."

"I don't believe he would ever have hurt her."

"You didn't live here at the time. You have no idea what went on. What people said at the trial."

"But —"

"They found him guilty."

Vivien nodded and stepped away. She turned back. "Mrs. Jenkins, are you afraid of Mr. Adair?"

The woman turned back and glared at Vivien. "How dare you. You're a child. Leave these matters to the adults. Excuse me." She walked down the aisle, turning at the end toward the desk.

I did it wrong, again.

Vivien made her way back to the table where Lauren sat reading. She'd finished all of the Jules Verne books the library owned and started reading H.G. Wells, as Vivien had.

The sound of raised voices came from the direction of the desk. Vivien figured Mrs. Jenkins was telling Mrs. O'Shea about their conversation. She became afraid. School would begin in about two months. At least Mrs. Jenkins wouldn't be her teacher this year. If only she could be in France by then.

TWENTY-ONE

D addy's letters still came once a week. He wrote about Fontenet and the French people. One letter recounted his time in Germany on TDY. The letter they'd been waiting for came in mid-July. He would leave France the first of October and arrive in Manchester either the second or the third.

"Have everything ready — packed or ready to pack when I get there. It will take a few days for the shippers to arrive. Once we are packed up, we'll drive up to New Jersey and pick up our port call."

"What's port call, Mama?"

"Orders telling us what ship to board."

"We're going by ship?"

"Yes, Daddy says it will probably be a troop ship. With lots of soldiers on board."

They now knew they wouldn't be flying to France. Going by ship would take eight days. Lauren looked forward in excitement to sailing on a ship. "It'll be such fun," she said.

"The weather will be rough that time of year," Daddy wrote. "But it will be a great adventure for the girls."

The first day of school came the day after Labor Day, meaning they would spend one more month at New Union.

"There isn't much to pack," Mama said. "But we should buy each of you a new coat. You've outgrown the old ones, and he says it will be cold on the ship and when we get to France."

They needed to go shopping in Nashville since Manchester didn't have much in the way of clothing stores. She could order out of the Sears catalog, but Vivien had gotten so much taller, she wanted to try the coats on before she bought them. When Lauren asked when they would go shopping, Mama said they would wait until Daddy came.

"We have to wait for him to get our shots, too," she said.

The need for shots ruined the exciting news. Vivien often threw up afterward. This time, she would be given an adult dose, which sounded worse. The only good thing? It would have to be done on school days.

The dog days of summer still lay ahead. Vivien didn't know the exact dates, but they started in July and ended in August.

"Mama, we can't wait 'til the end of August to go swimming again," Vivien said soon after Daddy's letter came.

"Please, Mama," Lauren chimed in.

"Let them go," Grandma said. "There hasn't been any more news about polio for quite a while."

"All right. Why don't you see if Emily and Jean would like to go with you."

The two friends came by several days before and asked if they could go, but Mama said, not yet. Vivien called and their mother said they would be right down.

"Glad to get 'em out of my hair for a bit," she said.

The girls changed into their suits, and their friends soon arrived. Emily brought the usual half a pack of L&Ms, and she and Vivien smoked while they walked around the curve and down the hill. Bushes and weeds blocked the trail a little more than the last time. Tennessee's weather was good for growing, and weeds could take over a space in no time.

Vivien stepped into the cool water. It didn't come up to her waist like before. The river level had gotten lower since the rainy season of spring and early summer, but high enough to enjoy a swim. The level would go down slightly more during the dryer month of August.

They swam and splashed water on each other. Vivien and Lauren told their friends about Daddy coming in October.

"We'll miss you," Emily said.

Her words surprised Vivien. They didn't spend much time together, not like the two of them did with Per and Karl in Breckinridge. Now that it came up, she knew she would miss the sisters, too. Making friends was difficult for her, unlike Lauren who always made friends easily. At the ford, it seemed they were all sisters. Besides, where would she get cigarettes?

Movement on shore to her right. She turned but Yoshi had gone, leaving Vivien with the feeling she watched from among the trees. She hadn't thought of the girl for several days, what with planning and packing, nor even looked over the scrapbook or cigar box. She felt guilty but didn't know what else to do.

She failed the girl she never knew. She didn't know exactly what Yoshi wanted, anyway. Well, she had a pretty good idea, if she thought about it honestly. It seemed any proof of Mr. McCarthy's innocence would be difficult to find. Since Yoshi remained unsettled, she felt certain Mr. McCarthy didn't kill Yoshi. He cared for her too much. The four girls who hassled the girl might have, whether all of them, she couldn't say.

Vivien stopped and listened. The other girls chattered.

"Quiet," she said. A roaring sound grew louder in the distance. Coming from upriver.

They all looked at one another. "Get out of the water," Emily said.

They rushed toward the bank. Vivien stood farthest away and when the others climbed out, she still had several feet to go. Vibrations in the water told her to hurry as Emily hollered, "Hurry."

She pushed ahead with her feet on the bottom and reached out toward the others. Emily grabbed one hand, Lauren the other. The next second, a rush of water hit her, nearly tearing her out of their grasp. Her feet came out from under her. Emily grabbed hold of a sapling to keep from sliding into the water. Lauren's hand slid from hers and Vivien swung farther into the flow. A tree branch glanced off her free arm. She slipped free of Emily's hold.

TWENTY-TWO

The water carried her several feet, and her head went under. The rush of water slowed as quickly as it began. The level dropped. Vivien splashed around until she got her feet under her.

"Are you okay?" Emily called out.

"Viv," Lauren shouted.

"I'm all right." She stood and brushed her hair out of her eyes, while she coughed and gasped for air.

"Do you need help getting out?" Emily asked.

"No, I can make it."

Vivien waded toward them. Her whole body trembled. She reached the bank, and the others grabbed her hands to help her out. Lauren spread a towel out on the ground for her to sit on. She'd swallowed water when she went under and couldn't stop coughing.

"That never happened before," Emily said.

Jean nodded. They both looked as shaken as Vivien felt.

The trembling eased up and the sun warmed her. "I'm all right," she said.

"Something must have dammed the river," Emily said. "A tree maybe."

Vivien agreed. Afterward, they sat quietly. When she felt strong enough, they started home. They said little, but it proved later an unspoken agreement existed among them to say nothing to their parents.

At home, they changed clothes. "How was it?" Mama called out.

"Great," Vivien said. She went out onto the back porch and sat in the rocking chair. She hoped Lauren would keep quiet about her nearly being drowned.

Yoshi must have caused the rush of water at the ford. Ghosts could do many things, like when Nurse Armstrong locked her in the hospital building at Breckinridge. How Yoshi managed to send a wall of water, she couldn't imagine, but it certainly wasn't a natural phenomenon.

Vivien pushed the rocker fast, and it creaked louder. Anger at Yoshi made her want to jump and shout, yet she hadn't the strength to do more than keep rocking. Why would the girl do such a thing? Vivien did what she could to find out whatever the girl wanted her to know. What she found convinced her of Mr. McCarthy's innocence, but with no proof. Neither of his innocence, nor of anyone else's guilt. She recalled the word used in one of the detective shows on TV: surmise. She only had surmises.

She stayed angry the rest of the afternoon and through supper. "What's got you so bothered?" Grandma asked.

"Nothing."

"Maybe you got too much sun today. You should go to bed early tonight."

Vivien nodded. She wanted to talk about what happened and . . . well . . . the whole situation. But she couldn't. It didn't help that Lauren kept looking over at her.

They finished dinner and the girls cleaned up the kitchen. Vivien fetched her book and tried to read out on the back porch where a light breeze blew. Darkness fell and the others joined her when their TV program ended. Grandma lit the lantern and set it on the porch rail to draw mosquitos and other bugs away. A few lightning bugs winked around the yard, but the season was passing.

Vivien, surprised by how tired she felt, went to bed first. She barely woke when Mama and Lauren came in. Her sister quietly slipped under the sheet. She slept again before Mama began snoring.

She woke in total darkness and sat up, listening. No clue what woke her, and now she heard only Mama snoring softly, and Lauren mumbling. Those sounds didn't bother her. No other sounds disturbed the night.

One of the roosters crowed. *Stupid bird.* At least he didn't wake anyone else.

She rose from the bed. Her bare feet felt the small tears and lumps in the linoleum on the floor until she stepped outside onto the uneven boards of the porch. Worn smooth by decades of people walking on them, the edges raised here and there, told her what part of the porch she walked on. The stars provided dim light to see by. She went to the post beside the steps and leaned with her arm around it and listened. No lightning bugs, so it must be late. The world wrapped her in fresh warm air. And silence.

Why were the tree frogs and bugs silent?

Someone's here.

Vivien backed away from the edge of the porch and stood against the wall, trying to be invisible and still watched. The outhouse stood darker against the horizon. The chairs against the wall of the house sat still. The trees behind the house and barn formed a black wall against the sky. The barn doors wide open formed a black square in the wall, like a mouth wanting to scream. All things she'd become accustomed to. A scraping sound came from the well house, open on three sides. Too dark to see anything there. The sound came again.

She looked down and listened for another sound. Startled by the near glow of her white baby doll pajamas, she realized anyone could see her.

She pushed away from the wall and moved toward the door.

"Grab her," a voice called out.

She reached out for the handle on the screen door. Strong arms grabbed her from behind and pulled her backward.

"Mama."

A hand pressed against her mouth. "Shut up and no one will be hurt." A man's voice, with a local accent. Strong arms picked her up and threw her over their shoulder. She bounced against the shoulder with every step he took, unable to catch her breath, much less scream. He hurried to a waiting car down on the dirt road, the engine running.

A car door opened and a figure got out. One assailant held her while they tied her hands behind her and tied a piece of cloth over her eyes. They tossed her onto the back seat. Her stomach hurt from the jostling against his shoulder and landing on the seat with all her weight drove the breath out of her. She sucked for air. Finally, she took a breath and exhaled.

"Lucky she came outside when she did," another man's voice said. She didn't recognize either voice. The third person hadn't spoken.

The car bumped along the road. She guessed it moved in the direction of the turnoff to the ford. No way to be sure. Lying on her side, her legs hanging over the edge, she pressed her feet against the floor so she wouldn't fall off the seat.

The car rounded the curve and turned left. It must be the

track to the ford. The car bumped hard several times, stopped, and the engine went silent. The front door opened, then the back door. The man pulled her out and set her on her feet. Her knees gave way. He grabbed her arm and held her until she could stand on her own. He held onto her while he bent down to pull something out of the car. She wanted to push him and run. Her hands were tied in front of her and she tried to push the cloth off her eyes but it was too tight. The car door closed.

The second man, now out of the passenger side of the front seat, took her other arm and they pulled her between them down the track. Sharp stones cut into the soles of her feet and she stubbed her toe on a large one. The glow of the light reached up to the canopy of trees bending over the track. Vivien wanted to look up at the men, but she needed to concentrate on her feet.

Even with the light from the flashlight, she couldn't keep up. She lost her footing, and they dragged her the last few feet. The sound of the river sounded different in the darkness. It grew louder until they reached the river's edge. She would swear it called her name.

Would she be drowned in the ford the same as Yoshi?

They stopped at the edge of the bank and removed the gag. "Can't we just tie her up and throw her in?" He sounded younger than the first man.

"It has to look like an accident or suicide. If she's tied, they'll know it's murder."

"Why are you —" Vivien said.

"Shut up," the older man said. "We'll have to get in the water with her and hold her under."

"I can't. She's only a girl."

"Do you want your wife thrown in jail?"

Wife? The younger man must be Buddy Dulaney, the philandering husband.

"Mr. Dulaney, please. Don't —"

The other man pulled her to him. "Be quiet."

"Why do you want to kill me?"

He pulled her along and stepped into the river changing the sound of rushing water. Dulaney stepped down behind him. They waded to the center of the river. "Now." The older man untied her hands. The glow of the flashlight lit up the river bank, throwing extended shadows behind the stones. He put his hand on the top of her head and pushed her downward. She gritted her teeth and tried to slip under his hand.

"Help me," he said.

Dulaney pushed on her forehead, and Vivien fell backward. She kicked and fought to get free. The older man released her head, and his fingers went to her throat. Vivien let herself sink below his fingers and away from Dulaney's hand. She kicked out, striking one of the men in the groin. He yelled, the sound distorted by the water. She kicked again, trying to swim away. The older man lost his balance and fell, his outstretched arm hitting her in the stomach. Vivien gasped and swallowed water.

She was drowning. She needed her feet under her. The closeness of the men prevented her from raising her head. A hand pressed against her stomach and pushed her down against the rocks.

She fought to hold her breath against the strength of the hand.

The weight of the hand disappeared, and she could move freely. She turned over and pressed her hands against the bottom, pushing herself to the surface, like Walt showed her and the other kids in the pool how to save themselves. She splashed at the water to get her feet under her and her head clear.

An arm reached under her and pulled her upward. She

fought against it, trying to swim away, but she had no more strength.

"It's all right," a man's voice said. A different voice. "You're safe."

Her body went limp. Coughing and choking wracked her body. The man lifted her in his arms and carried her to the bank.

CHAPTER
TWENTY-THREE

Vivien sat on a blanket, coughing and struggling to catch her breath. Someone wrapped another blanket around her shoulders. She couldn't stop shivering, like earlier in the day. Voices talked all around her. A man knelt down in front of her

"Are you feeling better?" he asked.

She nodded and looked up, surprised to see Mr. Logan. "What . . ." She cleared her throat and tried again. "What are you doing here?"

"The sheriff came into the newspaper office and we were talking when the call came from a woman asking for him. She shouted about someone being drowned at the ford. He'd come in asking questions about the drowning of the Japanese girl. I was putting tomorrow's paper to bed." He paused and looked around. "We can talk later," he said. "Right now, you probably need to get to the hospital for a check."

Vivien shifted so she could look around. Flashlights and headlights up the hill both lit the scene and cast long shadows. She recognized Sheriff Jameson, whom she'd seen around town a few times and during the problems at Grandma's house. He stood beside two men, with their hands handcuffed behind them like she'd seen on TV. She recognized Mr. Adair, Shelby's father, who she'd last seen helping to cut the wall from Grandma's house. She didn't know the other man, but guessed he must be her husband, Buddy. They brought her to the river and tried to drown her.

A blond woman stood by the two men, crying. Vivien recognized Shelby Dulaney when she turned to the older man. "Why, Daddy?" Mr. Adair said nothing. He must be the one who pushed her down into the water and tried to choke her. The blonde acted like she knew nothing about what happened, but Vivien felt sure she was the third person in the car. She turned away, too tired to feel anger.

"Vivien!"

Mama's voice called to her. The next moment, Mama knelt and wrapped Vivien in her arms and held her tightly. Hot tears welled up in Vivien's eyes and spilled down her cheeks. She sobbed, and Mama rocked her until she stopped.

"We'll take you to the hospital," Mama said.

The sheriff appeared beside them. "The deputy will take you."

A deputy carried Vivien because of the injuries to her feet from walking on and being dragged over the rocks. Mama kept a hand on her leg as they trudged up the hill to where half a dozen parked cars blocked the road. The deputy set her down in the back seat and Mama climbed in on the other side. She held her daughter close. They raced to the hospital in Manchester, the siren wailing.

CHAPTER
TWENTY-FOUR

The doctor on call examined Vivien. He found no lasting physical effects of the near drowning but wanted to keep her through the night. While he and the nurses worked on her damaged feet, Mama found a phone and called Grandma.

They also set up a cot for Mama who insisted on staying with her daughter. They settled down for the night, but Vivien couldn't sleep. When she closed her eyes, she felt the water, the hands pushing her, holding her down, and she cried out.

Mama sat on the edge of the bed and smoothed her daughter's hair back from her face. "Let's talk about it."

She propped Vivien up with pillows and listened to her explain about waking up and going outside. The two men grabbing her and carrying her to the car, then dragging her down the trail. "I'm sure Mrs. Dulaney was in the car. too. She never said anything." When she finished describing their horrible efforts to drown her, she began crying. Mama put her arms around her and rocked her. Mama cried, too. Gradually, Vivien drifted off to sleep.

Next morning, she woke early. The cot was empty, and Vivien lay back. Memories of the day before came back, but after a night's sleep, and sunlight coming through the window, fear passed away.

Soft sounds came from the hall outside the room. Nurses must be starting their rounds. Mama and breakfast arrived at the same time. Vivien felt hungry and she attacked the oatmeal and toast as if she hadn't eaten for days.

"I called your grandma and Lauren to let them know you are okay," Mama said. "It seems your sister may have let the cat out of the bag."

"About what?"

"About your nearly drowning twice yesterday."

"Oh."

"She didn't make much sense. She went on about a wall of water coming downriver."

"Yes."

"Why didn't you tell us?"

The doctor interrupted. He cheerfully examined her feet, advised her to stay off of them for a few days until they felt better, and told them she could go home. "Treat the cuts with mercurochrome or whatever you have," he said. "They're probably too painful for walking, but I'll tell you anyway. No walking around."

"How will I get around?"

"Does your grandma have a wheelchair?"

They both answered, no.

"Anyway, stay off your feet when you can. Wear socks to keep the wounds clean."

They promised, and the nurse came in to change the bandages before she left. After the nurse left, Mr. Logan appeared at the door.

"How are you doing?"

"She's all right for a person who nearly drowned twice in one day," Mama said. She clearly wanted to hear about the first incident.

"Twice?"

No time like the present. She explained about the rush of water coming down the ford and nearly carrying her away. She didn't say she suspected Yoshi did it.

"Oh, yeah," Mr. Logan said. "I heard about it and found out a farmer farther upriver partially dammed the river for several days so he could divert water into a new pond he'd dug out. More water built up than he expected and when he broke the temporary dam, the water rushed downriver. No one realized there might be people swimming."

Vivien laughed, relieved Yoshi hadn't tried to kill her. Mr. Logan asked if he could come to the house later and interview her about the kidnapping for an article. Mama reluctantly said it would be okay. He wished them well and left.

"You should have told me before about the water," Mama said.

"I know. But I thought..."

When she didn't continue, Mama said, "You thought it might be your ghost."

Vivien nodded.

Grandma and Lauren appeared, bringing clothes for her. They also brought a pair of sandals, but they wouldn't fit over the bandages. An orderly wheeled her to the hospital door in a wheelchair. Grandma's Ford sat outside and he picked her up and set her on the back seat. Mama drove home.

Vivien sat on the back porch with her feet up on a stool, wrapped in towels, resting on another towel, when she heard a car pull into the drive. She expected Mr. Logan but the sheriff appeared from around the corner of the house. Mama joined them. The sheriff asked questions while the woman deputy wrote down her answers. When he'd asked everything, the deputy shut her notepad, and the two rose to leave.

"I wondered if you might know who the little girl was last night," the sheriff said. "She stood on the side of the road and directed us to turn at the ford. I hadn't been that way for a long time, and she kept us from missing the turn."

Vivien shook her head. "I don't know. What did she look like?"

"Black hair. About your sister's size. She might have been Asian."

Vivien looked over at Mama, confused and disoriented. "Did you see her, Mama?"

Mama shook her head. Vivien told the sheriff she didn't know the girl, but she would thank her if they ever met. The sheriff thanked them and he and the deputy left.

Mama sat in the rocker and pushed it slowly. Vivien shifted her feet. The legs of the old wooden stool were uneven and it rocked.

"Your ghost, I imagine," Mama said.

In the next few weeks, details from fifteen years ago and the past few days came out. Shelby Dulaney, then Adair, and her school friends drowned Yoshi all those years ago. They'd only meant to taunt her, but it went too far. It turned out, Yoshi couldn't swim.

When Vivien began asking questions, Shelby panicked and told her father and husband. It seemed her father, determined to protect his daughter, ordered Buddy to go with him and "take care of the problem." Shelby's husband always did what his father-in-law told him to do.

"I'll bet they felt your coming out on the porch when you

did was a godsend," Mama said. She, Vivien, and Lauren sat on the back porch shelling peas from Grandma's garden.

"Something woke me," Vivien said. Was it Yoshi warning her of possible danger? It might have been the sound of the car, either the engine running or the doors closing.

"I wonder when Mr. McCarthy will be released from prison," Vivien said.

"It'll take a while," Mama said. "At least he's exonerated." She explained the word to the girls.

"I guess it's what Yoshi wanted," Vivien said.

The whole thing was crazy. She hadn't found proof of anything. Oh, Yoshi fed her the few scenes, but no one would believe it. Shelby Adair Dulaney had nothing to worry about. *Must have been her guilty conscience that made her panic.*

With a few weeks of summer left, school started the day after Labor Day. Daddy came the first week in October. Later that night, Vivien sat on the porch, enjoying the soft darkness and songs of tree frogs and cicadas. Soon, the heat and humidity would give way to cooler days. Her family would be gone by then.

Lauren had taken the lantern to the outhouse, and its glow showed around the ill-fitting door. The only light on the porch came through the back screen door. Mama and Daddy sat at the kitchen table, discussing the packing and how they would all make their way to New Jersey where they'd board the ship.

"I'm worried about what happened to Vivien," Daddy said, changing the subject suddenly. "I think she has too much freedom for a girl her age."

"I know," Mama said. "But you need to understand —"

"I don't understand. How can I. You haven't told me what makes her so special."

Special? I'm not special.

"It's a family thing," Mama said. "And a Southern thing."

"Superstition, you mean."

"Not exactly."

The discussion went back and forth. In the end, Daddy reluctantly agreed to let Mama handle issues with Vivien's conduct and safety. Mama agreed to tell Daddy if he needed to intercede. It was a huge concession on his part. He always wanted to be in charge, especially on matters concerning his family. Vivien didn't know whether to be glad.

The next week, the girls went to school while their parents packed, and made all the arrangements necessary for their move. Several trips were made to Smyrna Air Force Base to get their shots, tetanus, typhus, and several others.

Finally, their boxes and cases were picked up by a shipping company. The trailer was sold and moved. Grandma cried and hugged them all. She stood in the driveway, waving as they drove away.

They drove to the port in New Jersey, left the car to be shipped separately, and boarded the *U.S.S. General George M. Randall* troop transport ship to carry them across the Atlantic. In eight days, they would land in Bremerhaven, Germany, and travel by train, first to Paris, then to Fontenet, France where Daddy was to be stationed.

In all the excitement, thoughts of ghosts were replaced by the wonder of a ship full of military families and soldiers below decks, and the ship itself. The ship left the port in darkness without fanfare.

About the Author

Cary Herwig is an author of middle grade/young adult horror fiction. This is the second book in *The Army Brat Hauntings* series and Cary's thirteenth published book.

You can find Cary's blog at https://caryosbornewriter. blogspot.com/ and email her at iroshiok@gmail.com.

Also by Cary Herwig

The Army Brat Hauntings

The Ghost's Daughter

The World Ends at the River

Made in the USA
Columbia, SC
29 December 2023

29626953R00088